A DARK COFFIN

A DARK COFFIN

Gwendoline Butler

St. Martin's Press ⚏ New York

A THOMAS DUNNE BOOK.
An imprint of St. Martin's Press.

A DARK COFFIN. Copyright © 1995 by Gwendoline Butler.
All rights reserved. Printed in the United States of America.
No part of this book may be used or reproduced in any
manner whatsoever without written permission except in
the case of brief quotations embodied in critical articles or
reviews. For information, address St. Martin's Press,
175 Fifth Avenue, New York, N.Y. 10010.

Library of Congress Cataloging-in-Publication Data

Butler, Gwendoline.
A dark coffin / Gwendoline Butler.
p.   cm.
"A Thomas Dunne book."
ISBN 0-312-14577-2
I. Title.
PR6052.U813D37   1996
823'.914—dc20   96-25900
CIP

First published in Great Britain by Collins Crime,
an imprint of HarperCollins*Publishers*

First U.S. Edition: December 1996

10   9   8   7   6   5   4   3   2   1

A DARK COFFIN

1

It's all very well, all this sympathy with Jekyll, but what do you think it's like being Hyde – shut up inside all the time and only let out, escaping, when you can? And knowing all the time that you are fertile, and may breed worse than yourself.

Jekyll and Hyde and another Hydelet, eh? Well, think about it. And Hyde doesn't like Hyde's face any better than the world does. Hyde has eyes to see, and ears to hear. What Hyde sometimes lacks is a voice to speak.

All theatres have their own histories, their heroic moments, their tragedies, and their own ghosts. It is what gives them their colour, their character.

St Luke's Theatre in the New, the Second City of London, had a short history as a theatre, with not much chance to build up stories and ghosts. It was the creation of Stella Pinero, the actress wife of John Coffin, distinguished policeman, Keeper of the Queen's Peace in the Second City. Stella had had the idea of making a theatre here in her husband's bailiwick, and it had prospered. She had seen it grow from a small outfit to one which now had a main theatre, a smaller theatre workshop where more experimental productions could be mounted, and a fledgling drama school which worked in conjunction with one of the newest universities in the Second City. And soon, her theatre would have its own festival for two weeks in the summer. (After Ascot and Wimbledon and just as the schools broke up for their holidays.) The first festival was being organized and Stella was hopeful for a royal patron. Maybe a Princess?

But if St Luke's Theatre was new, it was housed in an old building. Stella had made use of an old church, bombed and fallen into disuse. She had rescued it from a future as a Bingo Hall. In the tower of the converted church, she and her husband had an apartment of great attractions with a splendid view towards the river, and perhaps less convenience if you lived up a winding staircase with rooms on every floor and a cat and a dog asking to be let out.

Coffin had received a quiet, unofficial backroom hint that the next Honours List could see him with a knighthood, but even if it was a life peerage, they would never move. It was so convenient being next to the theatre. You could almost say their marriage was founded on it.

St Luke's was a grey stone building, solidly constructed by its Victorian builder, who had been his own architect, with plenty of marble and decorative fretwork; it was not beautiful but it had charm. It had been built upon an older church, which had itself rested upon an Anglo-Saxon foundation. People said that a Roman temple had been the original holy spot whose dangerous powers had been exorcized by the planting of a church there by the early fathers of the English Church.

It was a workmanlike building, sitting upon the ground with some heaviness.

'It has such a comfortable, good feel, hasn't it?' enthused Stella. 'You feel so safe here.' She looked happily towards the stage which stretched out towards the audience with no sub-barrier. Stella belonged to the theatrical generation which had found the abolition of the proscenium arch exciting, so inevitably, when she had a theatre to plan, it had had to have a great apron stage stretching out into the audience which camped out all round it. Owing to the architecture of the church, two great pillars stood one each side or the roof would have fallen in, so there were created two boxes looking curiously royal. They were dark, and not much used as the sight lines were bad, and represented a problem. No one liked them. But Stella had seen to it that the seats in them were comfortable and were protected behind by a fretted screen. She called one the Royal Box, although no Queen had so far sat in it. The other box she called the Author's Box and there was a bust of Shakespeare in it, to prove it.

There was something about an empty stage which always excited Stella. 'Theatres can be spiritual places, can't they? We mustn't forget the origin of drama in religion. And this place was a church, after all. No wonder I feel St Luke's is good.'

If places could be good.

She was standing in the middle of the auditorium with her husband, John Coffin, beside her, and the theatre's general manager, Alfreda Boxer, on her right hand.

Stella looked taller and thinner since her recent session at a health farm where she had dieted and exercised. A film contract for a tall, thin lady with reddish hair was under discussion and Stella meant to have the part. Her husband found himself getting thinner out of sympathy; he was a tall, slender man in any case with bright blue eyes and hair now greying in a neat way. He was a neat man altogether who managed to make his clothes look good on him.

'Are places spiritual?' he asked now. 'A church must lay claim to it, I suppose.'

Alfreda looked thoughtful and said nothing. She thought St Luke's was hard work and might be a good place and might not. On that subject she was neutral. She thought places were neutral too, they were what you made them. This one paid her wages.

'That's why it's got no ghosts,' Stella went on.

'I don't believe in ghosts,' said Alfreda. 'Are you sure you do, Miss Pinero?' She always called her employer Miss Pinero, this being her stage name, although Alfreda well knew she was Mrs Coffin. She could have called her Stella, since the actress was not stuffy about that sort of thing and the theatre was more and more informal, but Alfreda herself felt more at ease with a bit of formality. It protected you somehow.

She kept her distance from John Coffin, because to her own alarm, she found him attractive. That way lay trouble.

Not that the Chief Commander had ever given any indication that he fancied her, or that his affections had

7

wandered from his wife. But they did say . . . but that was all in the past. Before Stella.

'How's the boy shaping?' he now asked in a jovial voice. He was finding that he dropped into a kind of false joviality with Alfreda which alarmed him. Why was he doing this? What was there about her? She was very attractive, certainly, and he was susceptible, but he had Stella now whom he loved.

'Fine, he's very happy.' Alfreda's son had graduated from drama school and was now an assistant stage manager at St Luke's. He was one of the reasons that Alfreda had taken the job of general manager for which she was, in some ways, overqualified. But keeping an eye on her offspring was a way of life with her. 'Well, I love him,' she used to say defensively, if she picked up any criticism on the lines of mother's apron strings, 'and I don't hang on to him.'

Coffin hesitated, as if he had forgotten the lad's name.

'Barney, plain Barney,' she said.

There it was again, that jesting, jousting tone, as if inviting battle. Inviting something, anyway.

'I don't think he'll ever make an actor but he might produce, or even write. He's dead keen on the theatre.'

Stella stopped admiring the stage (which she felt was her own creation), and turned her attention to Alfreda. 'Rubbish, don't downgrade him, I think he might make a very good character actor, he'll grow into it. Perhaps not do anything much until he's over thirty and then find his feet.'

'May I live to see it,' said his mother.

'I've seen it happen. And there's money in it.'

Coffin stirred with a touch of restlessness, unusual in him, but he had a lot on his mind, some problems, and he had been reluctant to take this tour round the theatre.

Stella picked up his mood. Understood it and sympathized, but he really must not brood. 'Let's take a walk.' They had been redecorating St Luke's and she wanted to see it. 'Decorators out?'

'Just.'

'They promised the end of last week.'

'Oh, you know how it goes. But they are good workmen.'

8

'Glad to hear it.' Stella was striding forward into the passage that led backstage. It was gleaming with new white paint. 'For what they charged.'

'We had a little bit of a flood where one of them left a tap running, no one admitted to it, but it must have been one of the painters.' There had been several little accidents lately, but she did not dwell on them. Accidents happen.

'They can pay,' said Stella firmly. 'No fire, or anything like that?'

'No fire. You'd have been told.'

'I think we would have smelt it,' said Coffin in a mild voice. His worry was eating inside him but he didn't want to show it. 'I sometimes think we can smell the greasepaint up in our tower.'

'No one uses greasepaint now . . . not much slap at all, it's all meant to look so natural.' Stella touched the paint. 'Not quite dry. Better be dry by the time we open.'

Alfreda followed Stella at a distance, letting Coffin get ahead of her. She had her own thoughts. In spite of Stella's words about this safe and comfortable old building, one or two of the girls had started to say things about not wanting to go through the corridors on their own, and not liking all the dark corners. There were a lot of dark corners. Getting darker by the day, some of them; the lights seemed to malfunction more than usual.

Coffin followed his wife in a dutiful fashion. Yesterday afternoon, a girl of eight had been knocked down and badly injured by a police car which was chasing a stolen van. Swinehouse was always a volatile and irritable district, so no one was surprised that a crowd had gathered quickly outside the Swinehouse police station. The mood had looked nasty, but a shower of rain had dispersed them before they got beyond shouts and threats. But he knew that the medical reports on the girl were bad, she might be permanently crippled if she survived at all. Since she was a popular little girl and her father was a local footballer, there would be more trouble when this got out. He had heard before coming out with Stella that the signs of trouble on the streets were there already in Swinehouse and could spread to other districts.

It was how the mood went, the report said.

In addition, the girl was reported to have a sweet singing voice which made her a local star. She might now have no voice at all.

He also had a slight problem with his wife. But he hoped he was more aware of that than she was. Imagination came into it. And there was one other ulcer gnawing away at his vitals.

Alfreda, striding by the side of Stella, decided that it would be better not to say anything about nervous actresses to her. Anyway, it was entirely possible she had picked up the stories too, she usually knew everything, and this was just her way of calming things down.

This is your day to be anxious and miserable, Alfreda told herself, take it, and cherish it and perhaps good will come of it. That was her philosophy of life at the moment, and it served.

She took a deep breath and walked on behind Stella. She wanted to be in a good mood because Barney would be home for supper tonight and her cooking depended on her mood, as she had discovered to her cost. Bad mood, burnt steak. Barney liked his food. Not a natural mother, she thought sadly, a natural mother would always cook well, no matter what her mood.

Behind them, in the Royal Box, the electrician was at work, testing the lighting in there. The bulbs in what he called 'that fucking box' seemed to burn out more than they should. Lately it always seemed to be darkness in that box.

He couldn't find anything wrong, so once again he replaced the light bulb.

Stella was on the stage itself now, where she always felt at home, and her husband was standing on the floor below, looking up at her.

'All right?' he said. 'Looks good to me.'

'Yes, I am really pleased with all the redecoration. It was generous of Letty to finance it.'

Letty was her sister-in-law, Coffin's half-sister, daughter

of their much-married, mysterious, long-dead (one hoped) mother with a taste for moving on and finding different spouses. Although whether she married them all no one knew. Coffin hoped not, because if so bigamy must have come into it somewhere.

Letty Bingham, also much married, was younger and richer than her half-brother. Very much richer at the moment (her capital wealth did vary from time to time, and crisis to crisis), having climbed back after a time of disaster during which Coffin had feared the worst.

'Least she could do.'

Letty had invested in the theatre and was a member of the Theatre Trust over which Stella presided.

Coffin followed the two women with as much patience as he could, while they continued the tour, inspecting the workroom where the scenery was prepared. He was always amazed how brilliantly the audience was conned into believing that bits of old wood repainted and rearranged from production to production, were a bit of the Roman senate, Hamlet's mother's bedroom, or Lady Windermere's drawing room. Or even, for that matter, the kitchen in *Look Back in Anger*.

The two moved on, inspecting the designs for the play currently on line: *Oh What a Lovely War*, which would be preceded, just to get the mood right, by a scene from *Journey's End*. He had thought himself that *Macbeth* might be a better play with which to celebrate the fiftieth anniversary of the end of the last war, but Stella had let her new young producer, Monty Roland, and his Young Theatre Group, have the choice.

'Just a quick look at the dressing rooms. I hope everyone is happy with them.'

'Oh, very pleased, Miss Pinero. And of course, having showers and hot water makes a big difference to them all.'

'So it should. I can remember having to change in a kind of barn, no water, not even cold, and walk across an open courtyard from the dressing rooms to the stage. Why do I say dressing rooms, we had but one, the sexes were separated by a curtain, which pulled across or didn't as the mood took us. But that was in Scotland and it was an old cowshed.'

And a long while ago, thought Coffin, but knew better than to say so.

He had come to support Stella and be part of her audience, but now he would like to get home.

Stella had nearly finished her inspection, by which she had been pleased. 'Came today just at this time on purpose,' she said. 'Not to get in anyone's way.'

Tomorrow the last frantic rehearsals began, today was a day off. Not that the theatre was empty, theatres rarely are, except in the small hours, and perhaps not then if the ghosts are out. Someone always seems to be around.

The wardrobe mistress was checking the garments for the dress rehearsal tomorrow and her assistant, Deborah, was ironing a shirt.

She rolled her eyes at Stella. 'The clothes those Tommies wore . . . I don't know what they felt like on, but they are bloody.'

'Don't swear,' said May Renier, automatically. Her face was flushed.

Deborah went on with her ironing. 'That wasn't swearing. And there *is* blood on this shirt . . . meant to be. It's the one the chap gets killed in.'

She held it up for Stella to see. 'Look, Miss Pinero, bloody, isn't it?'

But Stella had seen stage blood before, worn it once or twice, and was more interested in soothing her wardrobe mistress who was known to become a near hysteric (while pretending to be cucumber-cool) around final dress rehearsal time.

'How's it going, dear?'

'I believe we shall get through all right. Something will happen, of course, something always does, but we shall get through.'

You could almost hear May's teeth grinding. Coffin wanted to offer her a glass of water.

'We all know you suffer, May,' said Alfreda, without a great deal of sympathy.

'Your boy is looking for you,' May came back with, knowing where to strike.

'Where is he?'

'Looking for a knife, I think. He thought you might have one.'

'What for?'

'Well, not to kill himself or you, although I wouldn't blame him.'

Alfreda burst out laughing. 'What for?' She looked at Stella – Don't take any notice of us, just our game, and it helps May let off steam.

'He was going to cut a cake that Deb brought in.' She nodded towards a table in the corner on which a large white iced cake sat.

'Is it your birthday, Deborah?' asked Stella.

'Well, she isn't going to be christened or married, so yes,' said May.

'Where's he looking for the knife?'

May shrugged. 'On your desk, I expect, you seem to have everything else there, so we thought there might be a knife.'

'He won't find one there.' Alfreda went to the door and shouted down the corridor. 'Look in my handbag.'

'Knew you'd have one,' said May.

Coffin looked at Stella. They can keep this up for ever, his gaze said, and if we aren't lucky we shall have to stay and eat some of that cake.

Stella did the right thing, as she always did when it suited her. 'There's a bottle of champagne in my office. In the fridge. Send Tom for it and you three have it, with my love. Bless you all.'

She swept out, in her new blue and white Jean Muir, and Coffin followed.

In the corridor they passed Barney, plain Barney, who pressed himself against the wall politely so they could pass.

I think his mother beats him, thought Coffin, he always has a kind of bruised look.

'Rubbish, he's just young and nervous and in his first job,' said Stella, as if he had spoken aloud. Well, not quite his first job, he had worked on that stall that sold sandwiches and

13

hot dogs, but that was just to earn money as any student might.

'What did I say?' Coffin asked. 'Did I speak?'

'You said poor devil.'

'Would you want Alfreda for a mother?'

'She's devoted to him. You can see it. As he is to her.'

'I don't know about mother love, it never came my way.' Coffin's parent had dumped him early in life to be brought up by a woman he called his aunt, although their exact relationship continued to worry him. His memory let him down and the evidence was perplexing. Sometimes he told one story about himself, sometimes another. Meanwhile his mother had gone gallivanting off with numerous romantic encounters to her credit. If you could believe her own diary, discovered well after her death. If she was dead. The one truth about his mother was that you could not believe everything you heard.

No, he hadn't known much about mother love.

'And he has me as a guv'nor,' Stella finished triumphantly. 'He couldn't do better.'

She took him by the arm. 'Come on, they are not the only ones in need of comfort, you are. And there is some more champagne in our tower.' She looked in his face. 'Or you can have whisky or a hot cup of tea.'

'Do I look as bad as that?'

'Pretty well, love.' She put her arm round him. 'I know you are in trouble . . . Come on, let me bind your wounds.'

They walked the few yards to their tower.

'It's not just the child, although that's bad enough, nor worry about the riot – they probably have a right to kick up a stir,' said Coffin awkwardly, after a pause.

'No?'

He didn't say anything more, but took a deep breath.

'You want to answer or not?'

'I usually tell you everything.' Usually, but not quite always. I am not, for instance, going to tell you that I am sick inside about the man you met in Rome, Rome for romance, and who telephones you all the time. 'In the end.' It was a lame, doubtful finish.

'So not yet?'

'I think that's about it. Not yet.'

Too powerful, too horrible. Too much his. Not to be spoken of too soon.

'You're glum, that's what you are,' said Stella lightly, opening their front door, and stepping up the stairs. Right you are, her back said; her elegant swaying step said, I accept silence. Only not for ever. 'Glum and tense.'

'Not cross.'

'Very, very angry inside. I can feel it . . . Never mind, I don't mind a bit of tension in a relationship, it shows it's alive.'

She gave him a sharp look as if she might have doubted it otherwise. He did not respond.

Their living room smelt stuffy and hot, so Stella threw open the big sash window. The big tabby cat jumped on to the windowsill from the high branch of an overhanging tree and purred at her. 'You'll kill yourself one day doing that jump, cat. You'll get it wrong and fall.'

The cat ignored this, which he knew could never happen. Not to him. To the dog, possibly, or to another cat, but not to a brave cat. He knew that jump as well as he knew his name, and the certainty that, any minute, his mistress was going to give him his supper.

Coffin walked over to his desk. Amongst all the other communications, there was a message on his answerphone from the office.

'Harry Trent called from Greenwich. Inspector Trent. He will call again. He said it was personal.'

Stella, having fed Tiddles and also the dog, had returned. 'Shall we eat in or go out?'

He looked at her without seeing her.

'Answer, please.'

In a very little while, Stella's quick temper would show itself and that tension which she claimed to like in a relationship would prove itself very alive and very active. Boiling oil might come into it somewhere.

'Out.' Then he thought about Harry Trent trying to reach him on the telephone on some personal matter. 'No, here.'

15

And then, to hell with Harry Trent, out would be better. He liked Harry Trent, no question about that, a good man, and he had enjoyed working with him, but he was a man after whom trouble came trailing. Perhaps he was always so anxious himself. 'No, let's go to Max's.'

Over the years, the simple café with which Max had started out had flourished and altered its name from Max's to Maxi's and was now Maximilian's. Still Max's to Coffin, though.

'I'll just go and change, then.' Stella was cheerful at once. She loved changing her clothes, being in the theatre, putting on costume, taking it off, changing make-up was no hardship to her.

'Be quick then.' Or Harry Trent might slip in his call before they escaped. He wanted to escape.

'You could do with a fresh shirt yourself.' There was gentle but loving reproof in her voice, that rich voice that could express anything she wished it to.

But Harry Trent got in while he was still halfway clothed; he heard the bell and hoped she had not.

'Don't answer that,' he called to Stella. But she already had.

'It's for you.' And she handed him the telephone.

'Harry? Thought it might be you.'

'Is this a good time to talk?'

Coffin caught his wife's eyes, buttoning his shirt with one hand as he did so. 'Not too good.' But this was Harry, a man he had worked with and trusted. 'Make it quick.' But that sounded rough. 'Are you in trouble?'

'Difficult to talk on the phone. I need your help. Can we meet and talk?'

Coffin thought. 'Later maybe, I'll have to think. Things are complicated.'

'You mean about Swinehouse? I might be able to help you there.'

Coffin felt his eyebrows shoot up. What was Swinehouse to Harry Trent? And it shouldn't be. He was surprised, resentful and possessive. He hated the riot, at the moment, he hated Swinehouse, but it was his. What was Harry doing on his territory. 'Where are you?'

'Quite close. I'm having a meal at a place near you. Maximilian's, it's called.'

'Ah.' Ah, indeed. What was Stella going to say? 'I know the place. Hang on, will you?' He covered the phone while he spoke to Stella.

She was surprisingly understanding, and possibly even interested in Harry. Anyway, she made no opposition to meeting him.

'He can sit and watch while we eat, I suppose. And you can talk and I won't listen . . . there's bound to be someone there I know, there always is.' A good proportion of the floating population of performers working or rehearsing or just about in St Luke's Theatre ate in Max's. 'What's he in trouble about?'

'Don't know. But he seems to think it's one I can share in.' Or was it that Harry thought he could pass it on to Coffin?

'How well do you know him?'

'We worked together on and off on various cases when I was in Greenwich. He's much younger than I am and was a very junior officer. I got to know him a bit, not well, perhaps, but he was quiet about himself. Reserved, I suppose, didn't talk about himself.' He didn't really want to talk about Harry; he added thoughtfully: 'Not a happy man, but then he got married and that seemed to cheer him up. Or for a bit. But it didn't mean he talked more, he said almost nothing about himself and his wife. Unlike some.' But Coffin hadn't been a talker himself, so he understood that side of Trent. In a company of men, it was really better to keep a still tongue. Who said men were not gossips? Coffin knew better. 'But I liked him and trusted him. Yes, we were friends, but I was senior-ranking officer and that drew a line.'

Max's was crowded but Harry had a seat in the corner from which he could see the door and anyone coming in, so even if they had wanted to avoid him, it couldn't have been done.

He stood up when he saw them and waved his hand. That was Harry, discretion was not and never had been in his character. Coffin saw a man with broad shoulders, brown eyes and hair with no touch of grey. He looked as untidy as

Coffin remembered him, but he found himself glad to see the man and held up his own hand in acknowledgement.

Naturally Max, who had greeted them because he loved Stella and somewhat feared John Coffin, took it in. 'A table near your friend?'

Stella smiled, and Coffin realized with a pang that while Harry with his stocky figure and crest of hair might be no beauty, might be untidy, while his suit could do with a brush, yet the hormones were all there and what he did exude was a still-youthful maleness. Stella never minded that in a dinner companion.

'I'll go for a walk, then come back, I'd like a look round,' he said efficiently. 'Don't want to interfere with your meal.' Coffin remembered that Harry was always efficient.

'I'll disappear after we've eaten, and you two can talk. Several people I know here.' Stella looked round the room.

Harry rubbed his eyes. 'Don't mind if you stay. You might be a help.' Suddenly, he looked tired.

Stella decided. 'Then why don't you bring your coffee over here and you can talk while we eat?'

Coffin studied Harry's face, on which fatigue had left marks. Fatigue through work, which was common enough in police circles, or fatigue through something else? 'Have some wine with us.'

Harry rubbed his eyes again, as if there was some irritation behind them. 'Better not. I've been drinking whisky. I'll have some mineral water and coffee. Whisky makes me thirsty.'

Max told them what was best to eat that night and they took his advice: wild Scotch salmon, with cooked cucumber and salad.

'The food's good here,' said Harry. 'Not that I was in a noticing mood.'

'Clever of you to find Max's.'

'No cleverness . . . I was looking for you.' He rubbed his eyes again. 'It's about my brother.'

'I didn't know you had a brother.'

'You'd know it if you saw him: like as two peas, we are. Henry and Mark. It didn't matter which name we got, they

18

just handed them out. Twins. Two halves of one egg. He got called Merry, although God knows he never was.' Unless inside himself, he thought, he did have a secret laugh.

'I have a brother,' said Coffin, before he could stop himself. 'But I didn't know him, never met him or even knew he existed, until we were both adults.'

'Well, I knew mine from the minute I could open my eyes. Before, I daresay, in the womb.' He added with some bitterness: 'And we were not happy little boys.

'Too different, or too alike, I'm not sure. He hates me, I think, and I don't exactly love him. He said I sat on him all through gestation, and I daresay I did.'

'I don't like my brother very much,' said Coffin thoughtfully.

'We have such different lives; I went into law enforcement, and . . .' Harry hesitated. 'And he went the other way.'

'You mean . . . ?' Coffin felt his eyebrows shoot up.

'Yes, he's a criminal. Even the army couldn't control him, and chucked him out . . . I think he is wicked. He may be the most evil man I know.'

Stella was shocked. 'You don't believe in evil?'

'I do when it's in the family.' He sounded weary. 'And I only said may be . . . I always pray he isn't.'

Coffin said sharply, 'And you think he's in the Second City?'

'I think he is in Swinehouse,' said Harry simply. 'And if you are having trouble there, heaven help you, because he is probably behind it. In there driving it forward.'

'And why do you think he is here?'

'Because we were fostered as kids for a while, just a short while with a couple called Macintosh, strict, rigid even, but it suited him somehow; I think he has come back.'

Coffin thought about it. 'He kept in touch with them then?'

'He never kept in touch with anyone in his life.'

'So what makes you think he's here?'

'I saw him on TV. On the news, at the riot, he was laughing.'

'I see. Thanks for telling me. You're sure?'

'I know his face. I see it every time in the mirror when I

shave myself . . . He might be staying with the Macintoshes. If he is here, he came because he remembered them.' There was something heavy in his tone.

'And you don't like that?'

'No.' A bleak, cold monosyllable.

Coffin thought about it. 'So what's he running from?'

Harry dropped his head and looked at the table. 'I dunno . . . maybe murder. He could have killed a woman in Woolwich. Strangled her and left her on Woolwich Common. He says not, but he would, wouldn't he?'

'I don't know, Harry, he's your brother. Did you believe him?'

'I never believe a word he says.' But Harry kept his eyes fixed on the table.

'Look at me, do, Harry.' He looked up, his eyes blind. 'And? Come on . . . And?'

'I'm worried for the old couple. How do I know what he wants? He may harm them. He is dangerous.'

A couple called Macintosh lived in Swinehouse, Joe and Josie who ran a mobile fish-and-chip van. They also served hamburgers, sausages, fried chicken and toasted sandwiches. With tea and coffee to drink. All good, all fresh and tasting well. They were popular local figures who were welcomed as they toured the streets of Swinehouse where eating houses were hard to come by. They regularly parked in spots around the theatre. Even Coffin ate there sometimes when Stella was away and he wanted a quick meal, and he was sure that Bob, their dog, hung about the van when he could get out on his own, while the cat probably ate there regularly when fish was frying. The cat was an animal with a strong character and a habit of roaming in search of good food.

Josie cooked and Joe served, except that sometimes the positions were exchanged and Joe cooked and Josie served – they were interchangeable. Josie was tall and thin, Joe was just as tall and very nearly as thin. They bounced jokes off each other like two old comedians.

The van was always parked in the shed beside the house in Tolliver Street. Once vandalized, the neighbourhood took such strong revenge on the lad that did it, that it was never again touched. Tolliver Street itself had changed radically since the Trent boys had lived there. Once a row of small houses, only the Macintosh house remained. On either side the rest had been replaced by blocks of flats. The Macintosh house, which had once, long ago, been a livery stable, sat in the middle of its own freehold.

The Macintoshes were nice, gentle, quiet people who were always very circumspect with the world outside and each other, as if they had been badly hurt once and were on the lookout for when it happened again.

That night, when Coffin was talking to Harry Trent, and while a tall man was just about to throw a brick through the window of Tallow Street Police Station, the Macintoshes' van was parked near the theatre where it was doing a good trade in hot sandwiches, in spite of the heat of the evening.

This was not their usual beat on a Wednesday night, but the Macintoshes knew enough to keep away from Tallow Street where the crowds were gathering.

'We've always managed to keep out of the rain, haven't we?' Josie nudged Joe.

'It's going to be a bloody thunderstorm this time, loved one.' Joe was usually the gloomier of the two. 'Pass me the sausages.'

Josie handed them over. 'It can't be that bad, can it?'

'Guess it could be, lover.'

'No, no, I won't believe. We are imagining things.'

Joe did not answer, he just got on with cooking the sausages. 'We could always get out,' he said at last.

'Get out? Do you mean what I think you mean?'

He turned the sausages in the big pan. 'Yes. Not such a bad thing. Out.'

Josie was buttering the rolls. 'Are we in the firing line then, Joe? No, I won't believe it.'

Joe didn't answer, just went on with the sausages, and Josie remembered something else.

'Joe, do we know someone called Merry? He wants to come round. Left a message on the answerphone.'

*   *   *

21

Coffin sat over his wine with Harry while Stella tactfully took herself off for a theatre gossip with some cronies across the room. She knew when to make herself scarce.

'They were decent enough people, the Macs, although they had a tough side, you kept their rules. They ran a small ice-cream van in the summer and fish and chips in the winter.'

'I think they still do something similar,' said Coffin thoughtfully.

'Do they? Thought they might have retired by now.'

'No, not yet. Gone upmarket, I'd say.'

'Really? You surprise me. Didn't seem that sort.'

Coffin leaned forward. 'Your brother, what do you want done?'

Harry looked thoughtful. 'Dunno.'

'I could bring him in, I suppose. If he's been in the riot, have him charged.'

Harry had sorted himself out a bit. 'I think I just want to lay hands on him before he does something terrible . . . I know I am a grown man, and so is he, and we are both responsible for our own actions, but I feel as though I am responsible with him, as if he is a part of me. Or I am of him.'

He looked at Coffin and spread out his hands. 'Twins are different.'

'They must be. Does he feel the same about you?'

'No, I don't think so, but I'm not sure. It may be because I went into the police, he became what he is, perhaps couldn't help himself. You don't believe that?'

'And I don't think you do.'

'Some of the time, oh yes, I do. The worst times.'

'What's his record? Come on, you can tell me. I can find out.'

Harry trotted a sad, bitter little list of shoplifting, robbery, succeeded by robbery with violence.

'Has he ever killed anyone?'

Harry took a deep breath. 'I think he did once. The girl that I told you about, but it was never proved and he always said No, not him.'

22

'That's the worst, is it? There's nothing else I ought to know?'

Harry seemed to debate inside himself. 'We're still close, not telepathy or anything like that, but I like to know where he is and what he's up to. And sometimes I pick up feelings, sensations . . . I don't know if he is the same way with me, it was so when we were kids, but that was a long time ago.'

He waited for Coffin to laugh or crack a joke, which was why he never admitted any abnormal closeness with his twin in the society of policemen in which he moved. Probably wouldn't admit them anywhere, he told himself, but it seems necessary now.

'And now you have a bad sensation?'

'Horrible,' said Harry frankly. 'Like knowing you've got a mortal disease . . . I think he is my mortal disease.'

Coffin stood up. 'I think we need a stronger drink, both of us. I will see what Max can do, and I ought to make a telephone call.'

Trent nodded. 'I suppose I ought to call the wife.'

'There are two phones here. A fax as well. Max has everything. How is Louise?' He had to work to remember her name.

'Fine,' said Harry without notable enthusiasm.

'How are things?'

Harry pulled a face. 'Not one of those failed police marriages, if that's what you mean . . . It works, she goes her way and I go mine.'

Coffin remembered that Louise was a career woman. 'She's not in the Force too?'

'No, nothing like, miles away. She's a solicitor.'

'Not such miles.'

Harry laughed. 'Don't you believe it. She's part of what's called a Citizens' Legal Agency, me and mine are the people she fights against. We're dirt in her book.' He gave Coffin a wry look. 'Businesswise, of course. Nothing personal.'

Not a lucky man, Coffin thought. He nodded towards the end of the room. 'Phone's over there.' As he did so, he caught Stella's interested gaze. She had probably been doing some lipreading.

They went off to their separate telephones to stand, side by side, backs to the room.

Stella looked at them and shook her head. You could see they were both coppers, she thought, from the way they stood. Coppers or villains. The steam of the world in which they moved had blown over them both. She went over to them.

'Tell me,' she said. 'Do you remember anyone called Merry? He wants to come round. He's left a message with Max.'

Merry, as he walked, was thinking: he's close, somewhere around here, I can smell him. He's coming out, that's what it is. It's like an old familiar smell. I suppose I hate him. Or does he hate me? Maybe the same thing. I'll track you down, Harry, we have a score to settle, and we will. That's a promise. From me to you.

And then he said aloud, so that all of Shambles Passage could have heard if it wished: 'Doesn't he realize what a sham his marriage is?'

Back at the theatre, the electrician had finished his work and gone home.

The lights in the box on the prompt side worried him. They were working tonight, but dim.

There was too much darkness altogether in that box, he didn't understand it, but he didn't like it.

'I'm a practical man,' he said to himself. 'But there is something wrong here.'

Coffin finished his telephone call first and went back to his table. Stella walked over.

'Good news or bad?'

'Middling. Jim Tanner is in charge and says he's controlling it, and I'd better keep away.'

Superintendent Tanner of the uniformed police was a good and efficient officer. And also tactful.

'He didn't put it like that.'

'No, but he let me know I might just inflame them down

there if they saw me and certainly get the media.' Which in turn would have its own inflaming effect, probably. 'They have got a camera going. So we shall see who's there.'

'You mean Harry's brother?'

'Do I?' said Coffin blandly. 'Harry, how's things?'

Harry Trent sat down, he looked more cheerful. 'Lou's all right. She sort of gave me her blessing on coming here. She's blamed me more than a bit for what Merry is, also she had her own advice as it happens, she thought I ought to look up the Macintoshes.'

'Will you? You can put up with us if you like?' Coffin looked at his wife, who still owned an apartment in St Luke's, used it as an office, but did not sleep there.

'Sure.' Stella smiled. 'You can have my flat for the night or so . . . I'll let you have the key. Walk round with us and I will show you the place.'

'I'd like to, thanks.' He gave Stella an appreciative look. 'Lou says I'm housetrained.'

'You can call round on the Macintoshes.'

'I have tried. The house is still there but no one answered the bell. It's all changed round there.'

'I expect they were out selling hot dogs.'

'I'm surprised they are still at it.'

'Come to the theatre tomorrow with us, they will be outside.' Stella had decided she liked the man.

'I'd like that . . . Have a drink with me first, here . . . No, come to the flat, your flat, I'll do some shopping and we can have a drink and some sandwiches.' He did not add 'in the quiet', but might have meant it, because Max's was hotting up with some younger members of the theatre staff, laughing and talking.

Max never minded, he encouraged voices and laughter, but it had to cease before midnight.

At home, Stella and Coffin prepared for bed in companionable silence. Out of the corner of his eye, he saw Stella's shape in a soft apricot satin nightgown and enjoyed it. But he said nothing.

'Well?' said Stella. 'What are you thinking?'

25

'Partly about you.'

'And partly about Harry Trent? Don't you like him? I wondered.'

'We were very close at one time; he nearly got me killed.'

'That doesn't seem a reason for closeness.'

'Oh well, I nearly got him killed too, we were in it together . . . too close to a pair of villains with guns. And unprepared. As much my fault as his. More really, since I was the senior by a long way.'

'So, what's the trouble?'

Coffin was silent, he sat on the edge of the bed. 'What did you make of him?'

'I liked him. Why?'

'I'm not sure if I believe his story . . . I never heard about the twin before. I suppose there is one.'

'What an extraordinary thing to say.'

'Might be an excuse.'

'What for?'

'I don't know. Excuses are always useful.' Good excuse for a lot of things if you can bring it off.

While they were talking, the watchman who walked through the theatre slowly, carefully at night, checking for intruders, came into the auditorium. By the low security light which was always on, he could see it was empty.

He paced on round. No one.

He stood still for a moment and looked around. Still no one.

He walked on, looking at intervals.

Why did he have this feeling that someone was about?

In the shadows, a dark figure flitted away.

Evenings when a new show opened were always a cause for celebration at the St Luke's Theatre. Each new production was a rebirth.

This particular evening was no different, Stella was happy and excited, she always was, while her husband went with her because he enjoyed her company and had to admit that he liked the theatre. Stella had said to him once that he was a

26

closet tragedian, but he had settled for being a lost comedian which seemed more desirable for a policeman somehow.

Especially for a policeman who had the riot police out two nights running. Last night, thank God, had been quieter, and if Harry's brother had been around, he had not been noticed. But Coffin now had his address in Swinehouse, knew where he was staying, or a man who fitted the description, although not why, and the owners of the house had received a quiet warning from Sergeant Fraser who claimed to know them well. Coffin was now debating whether to tell Harry or not.

They had met Harry for drinks first. As promised, he had done some shopping so that he could offer them a good white wine, as well as smoked salmon sandwiches. All courtesy of Max.

'What's the day been like?'

'Bearable, just about.' Coffin sounded weary, so that Stella gave him a sharp look but said nothing. 'You helped us there in identifying your brother.' He saw Harry wince. 'It's all right, he wasn't arrested, in fact, he hasn't been back to where he was lodging, he may have cleared out.' Harry did not look relieved but Coffin went on: 'So, not too bad a day.' The streets were quiet but not peaceful, there would be trouble again if the child died and the news of her condition was not good.

'I had a look round, wondering if I could find Merry. Didn't.' He looked at Coffin.

'I can give you his address in Swinehouse,' said Coffin slowly. 'Or where he was. An old seamen's lodging house. Or it was when the river had seamen on it, now anyone can live in it. Mother Arbatt's, is the local name, two, Shambles Passage . . . there used to be an abattoir in the passage when cattle came in live from Canada . . . long gone, of course, but locals say you can smell it on a hot day. Not sure if you would be wise to call, not one of the best houses in the world.'

'It wouldn't be if they let Merry live in it.'

'He's been living there for some weeks.' Registered, anyway, but not seen much. A popper-in, you might say, rather than a continual inhabitant.

27

'I'll go tomorrow.'

Coffin nodded, watching Stella quietly mopping up the mess where the wine had dribbled on to a good table. It was her table, after all. 'Up to you.'

'I told you I went to see the Macintoshes yesterday. Found the house, all changed of course, with flats on either side.' Must be a valuable site, he had thought, but the house looked run down. 'They weren't there. Out with the van, I suppose. I saw where they parked it. I tried to track it down but couldn't find it . . . but I may see them tonight. They are going to be at the theatre.'

'How do you know?'

'Max told me . . . I was talking to him when I bought the wine . . . Said someone had made them a present of some tickets and they were going.'

'Max always knows everything,' said Stella. 'He is very helpful.'

'When it suits him.' Coffin had made it his business to find out about Max since he was now so much a part of his wife's business life with the way he ran the theatre catering – very well, it must be said. Coffin wanted to know. Max had come to England from Northern Italy as a young lad, after the war; he had come on his own, with no money, to make his fortune, which he was in a fair way to do. Coffin reckoned he would die richer than the Chief Commander himself ever would. Starting in a small way, Max was getting richer.

Stella was practical. 'Will you know the Macintoshes again after all this time?'

'I think so, unless they have changed a lot, but they will look older. Max said that they told him someone had given them a box.'

'Oh, that will make it easy, there are only two boxes. One on each side of the stage between pillars of the old church that could not be used. The sight lines are poor but you can hear well.'

'I'm surprised there are boxes . . . I thought it was a theatre in the round.'

He'd been doing his research, Stella thought with amusement.

He read her mind. 'I'm interested in the theatre. Like to have been an actor, I know I couldn't have been, no talent but the interest is there. Unusual in a copper, I suppose.'

'What about me?' Coffin had the feeling he was being left out.

'You married into it.'

'I married you, Stella,' Coffin observed mildly. 'Not the theatre.'

'Same thing. I wonder if you would have married me if I hadn't been an actress.'

'But you wouldn't be Stella,' he said unanswerably and honestly.

Stella looked enraptured. She came over and kissed him. 'You angel . . . you do know the right things to say.' Then as she drew away: 'Mind you, I've told you before that you are a bit of an actor yourself.'

Then she turned her attention back to Harry, and Coffin wondered once again about the man in Rome. American, wasn't he? Probably not a bit important to Stella but he wished he was sure. That kiss just now, not like Stella as a rule, she played it cool in public. Perhaps she felt she owed him something.

'I can feel evil,' said the nightwatchman to one of the ushers. He intended to stay to see the performance: not only an old performer (in a humble way, an extra at Elstree, a chorus boy, a man who walked on), he had also fought in the war. He wanted to see.

'Oh, come on with you, Albie,' said the usher. 'There's Miss Pinero coming in with her husband and a friend. No evil when she's around, she wouldn't allow it. Keeps the discipline, that one. And look at her smile, such a happy smile.'

'Fool,' muttered the old man. 'Evil has nothing to do with discipline or a happy smile. It's like blood, you can smell it.' All the same, he smiled himself at Stella as she went past in a gust of Jolie Madame. 'Evening, Miss Pinero.'

*   *   *

They were late to the theatre. 'Excuse me,' said Harry, disappearing. 'Won't be a minute.'

Stella and Coffin waited. Weak bladder, Stella thought. She had a performer's bladder herself and felt no discomfort till the show was over.

Harry returned with an apology – 'Sorry' – and followed Stella as she led the way to their seats and although Harry Trent looked around him, he didn't see the Macintoshes.

'Already in their seats.' Stella led the way to the special house seats always reserved for her and her friends.

The young and ambitious producer, Monty Roland, had decided to make his mark on the world with this production: there would be no interval (something no management liked because it cut down bar profits, but he was too young to think this mattered or was any concern of his), it would break the mood, but the pace would be fast and there would be a party afterwards.

For celebrities, critics and his friends.

Harry was looking around him as they settled in their seats, but the lights were already being lowered, slowly shade by shade, so that people seemed to recede into the shadows. 'Can't see them, can't see into the box.'

'Perhaps they are in the other box, on the prompt side.'

Harry did not know which was the prompt side, but he could see into one of the boxes which was full of teenagers. 'No, I can see into that one, and it's not them. Their grandchildren maybe, if they have any.'

The other box was very dark, but there might be two figures sitting there. Yes, there were, you could just make out the shapes. Harry relaxed a little.

'Oh, grandchildren, had they, do you think?' Stella was always interested in personal details, it was one of the things that made her a good actress, because she carried within herself a compendium of people's behaviour, their relationships, desires, ambitions, loves and hatreds. She had this reservoir to call upon when required to build a part.

'I believe there's a daughter.'

Stella was clearly about to ask about the daughter, but all

the lights went out, and heavy, complete darkness descended upon the theatre.

It lasted for a long moment, then a distant thunder of artillery fire.

Then silent darkness again and the Last Post sounded.

The curtain went up on a trench in Flanders, World War One.

'I don't know anything about that, she may be dead,' said Harry hastily to get his word in before the action started on stage. He looked at his programme and fidgeted a little while Stella smiled at her neighbour on the other side, an actor she knew and had played with but who was currently out of work.

Harry turned to Coffin. In a low, uneasy voice, he said: 'I feel as though my brother is here. I can sense him.'

'Oh, come on. You always were one for a bit of a rigmarole, Harry. I remember when we worked together and I used to enjoy it. But now . . . look around. Can you see him?'

'I don't need to see him,' muttered Harry as the actors began to speak.

Coffin did his best to attend to the performance, it was a duty that Stella expected of her spouse, but his attention kept wandering. He found he enjoyed the extract from *Journey's End* more than he expected but after that he went back into his own thoughts.

No interval, unluckily, but he would telephone to find out how the girl was holding up the minute the show ended. If there was any trouble on the streets the message would get to him anyway. He had left instructions on that score.

As the curtain came down to enthusiastic applause from the audience, which Monty had carefully packed with friends and relations, Stella leaned across to Harry. 'Wasn't bad, was it? I think Monty might develop very nicely. He's a bit mannered now, of course.'

'You mean the soldiers in underpants?' said Coffin.

'That was just to show they were dead, Monty wanted shrouds or naked, but I said not.'

'I think you were right.'

31

Stella ignored this. 'Harry, Monty's having a party backstage to celebrate, we must all go. You'll enjoy it.'

But Harry had his eye on the box in which he could see two figures still sitting.

'I want to see the Macintoshes first.'

Coffin said that he would come too, he would take the chance to see if there were any messages for him. No riot tonight, or he would have been plucked from his seat already.

Stella was moving ahead out of their seats and down the aisle, greeting people as she passed. 'See you at the party, then.'

Coffin and Harry together made their way to the back of the box. There was no door as such, but a low balustrade which opened.

Two figures were there, in their seats, but one lolled against the other whose head was flung back.

Coffin stopped and put his arm on Harry to hold him back. 'Wait . . . something wrong here.' He went through into the box, and looked down upon Joe and Josie Macintosh.

Joe stared back with open, sightless eyes. He was quietly dead.

The movement of air caused a small piece of paper to flutter to the ground. Coffin bent down to pick it up.

Coffin wondered what it was, but at that moment he did not realize it had two functions.

One was: a message from Hyde out of Jekyll. Hyde was out and walking round and Jekyll did not yet know.

Not for sure, that is, but Jekyll had suspicions that the enemy was loose.

2

Coffin held the piece of paper in his hand; he had picked it up carefully using a folded envelope from his pocket as a kind of pincer. Such behaviour was automatic with him. Fingerprints, they might be important, you never knew. He hardly thought about it, just did it, always the policeman.

It was a sheet of writing paper, a little dirty, almost as if someone had trodden on it. One corner was bent over. Several lines of writing in pale ink were to be seen.

He glanced at it quickly. 'It looks like a suicide note.' He did not hand it over to Harry who had pressed into the box by his side, and was staring down at the two figures. There was not much room but the low door had been pushed apart so Harry could get in. Behind him a small, interested crowd of theatregoers was gathering.

Coffin waved them back. 'Go away, please, just leave, there has been a death here.'

He turned to Harry. 'You stay here and keep people out while I get things moving . . .' He moved away quickly, pushing the small crowd in front of him. Alfreda had appeared, together with Barney, she gave Harry a quick look, Coffin motioned her to follow him, talking rapidly as they went, explaining what he wanted her to do: clear the area as quietly as possible, keep the audience there if she could but if not get the names and addresses of people as they left, but to hang on to all those with seats near the box. And the performers and theatre staff must stay, of course. Yes, he said, it appeared to be a suicide pact but they must make sure.

'I understand.' Alfreda nodded, Barney, full name Barnabas, only used when he was in disgrace, stood by her side, wide-eyed and interested; he had never seen death before and now he was getting a double dose. He found it absorbing, worth observing, almost like a show. One of the bodies, Joe it was, leant against the other as if asleep, while Josie, he thought it was Josie but oddly he got them mixed sometimes, lay with her head sagging back. You could see at a glance that he—she was dead, while Joe might have been asleep.

'Are they really gone?' he asked, but no one answered. He was Barney – not important. His mother tugged at his arm to pull him away.

Harry watched them go. Get things moving, he thought, wouldn't it be better to get everything stopped? He groaned inside himself. Too late, far too late.

I cannot believe what I am seeing, he told himself. I can't believe my own eyes.

The squad car arrived with a uniformed man and woman, to whom Coffin spoke.

'Where is that police surgeon?' he demanded. 'I want these bodies moved.'

So did Alfreda who had returned to hover in the background, anxious and pale. Stella stood by her with Monty, who was silent and angry. How could anyone die on his first night?

'Who is the surgeon?'

'Dr Mason, sir,' the policewoman answered. 'Dr Margery Mason.'

Coffin nodded; he knew Marge; she did a good job, sometimes in unpleasant circumstances on odorous and difficult corpses but always behaved with gentleness to the dead, long dead although they sometimes might be.

Tonight would be a comparative treat for her, he thought. When she arrived. If she had a fault, and he recognized it was a small one, she was tardy.

'She's on her way, though, sir,' said the policewoman, who also knew Dr Mason and perhaps guessed his thoughts. 'She already had a floater down at Craven Creek but she called in to say she was coming. The creek's not far, sir.'

Dr Mason was wearing a smart evening dress when she arrived, but she showed no anger at having been called away from her dinner party by two incidents on the same night.

She looked surprised to see the Chief Commander there, this was top brass indeed, but she acknowledged to herself that this was his wife's theatre and did not allow his presence to break her composure as she knelt to make her inspection.

'Well, they are dead. I can certify that. Exact cause as yet to be established. If there's a suicide note, I will make a guess at a drug of some sort.' She rose to her feet, giving Joe and Josie a thoughtful look. 'They seem peaceful enough, but you can't tell. Perhaps a faint look of surprise on the man's face. The postmortem will tell more.'

She would not be doing that. 'I suppose Dennis Garden will fall for this . . . he's just back from a holiday in Spain.'

'He ought to be in an easy mood then.' Coffin was not an admirer of Mr Garden, too bossy by half, a man of self-importance, but he admitted the man was the total professional.

'He's very good,' said Marge Mason loyally, picking up her bag.

They both knew she hated his guts. Dedicated and determined homosexual as he was, he had made a single-minded play for her boyfriend.

She shouldered her bag and made for the door. Geoff was loyal, thank goodness, no doubt about that, but all the same . . .

She turned back for a look again at Joe and Josie. Something was worrying her. 'Who are they? Have you got a name?'

'Macintosh.'

She frowned. 'I feel as though I know the faces. Of both of them.'

'I expect you do, if you ever bought a hamburger or an ice-cream from their stall,' said Coffin.

'Leave you to it then, sir.'

'Be off myself as soon as the CID team turn up.'

In the ordinary way Sergeant Davis and DC Armitage might not have hurried themselves to a suicide, but a suicide in the Pinero Theatre and the presence there of the Chief Commander and his wife meant that they were walking in

35

even before Marge Mason had left, and were perhaps a little put out that she had got there first.

'Better try wings next time, boys,' she murmured quietly as she walked past. 'I'll be sending in a report, looks like double suicide. The boss knows all and is waiting for you. Good luck.'

'Come on,' said Coffin wearily to Stella, after a few words with Davis. 'Let them get on with it, not my job, and they don't want me here.' It had been his job once, which the two CID officers knew, just as they knew what his reputation for efficiency and flair had been.

'All right, love, just let me have a word with Alfreda.'

She turned towards Harry Trent who was standing there in silence, looking white. 'This can't be good for you, you knew them.' He muttered something wordlessly about it being a long while ago. 'Forgive,' she said, with one of her famous smiles. 'Back soon.'

To Alfreda she said: 'Sorry to leave you to it. Monty can't have his party. It wouldn't be tactful. The bodies are still here.'

'He wants it, of course. Says all this is nothing to do with him, and the food will go off.'

'He's got no judgement. Tell him he can have it tomorrow and bother the food, Max can do some more.' As, for a price, he would. 'I'm afraid you are going to have to hang around until the police go. Take your line from them.'

Alfreda nodded. 'Barney will stay with me.'

'Good lad,' said Stella, once again distributing her famous smile.

With knobs on, as Barney said cynically to himself, even as it warmed him. 'I'll stay with Mum, of course I will.' He had to admit to himself that it was interesting and that he was enjoying himself.

He placed himself protectively by his mother. He was a lanky lad, as tall as she was, with bright blue eyes and a crest of reddish hair. Otherwise they were not alike, and he prided himself on taking after his dead father. If he was dead, he cherished the idea that what Alfreda had told him of the death in an accident was a lie, and that Dad would turn up, rich and famous. He had to be both or need not bother acting Lazarus.

'Remember what old Albie said about feeling there was someone around who shouldn't be?'

'The nightwatchman? He talks too much, I've thought so before,' said Alfreda gloomily. 'I ought to sack him but I can't bring myself to do it.'

'Think he'll tell the police?'

'Bound to. If he gets the chance.' Alfreda was keeping her eyes on the police pair, she couldn't hear what they were saying, but they didn't seem too anxious. A death was a death, this didn't look too important to them. 'I think we will be on our way soon. I think the police will let us go quickly, we aren't important. I'll tell Monty about his party, but I must have a drink first, he can wait. He's stalking about like a cross cat as it is; let him stalk.'

'Think we ought to stop Albie talking?'

'Can't be done. If he wants to, he will.' She yawned. 'No one takes him seriously. That pair won't. You can tell by the way they are going about things that they like routine up and down and all the time, and no trouble.'

'We ought to let him,' persisted Barnabas, he felt a slight touch of the Barnabas syndrome coming on, but he was trying hard not to let it happen. Disgrace is thy name, Barnabas boy. 'Only decent.'

'Decent? What a word, I'm having none of it.' She yawned. 'Bloody awful evening it's been, hasn't it? And Monty's production wasn't that good either. Come on, we'll go round the theatre and check up, then see if we can slip away home.'

She stalked off with what Barnabas called her Lady Macbeth walk. I am always Barnabas when she is like that.

Barnabas followed, wondering: If you opened up my mother, if you could, and called Come out, come out, I wonder what would come out?

Death was so close and she wasn't giving it due dignity.

He said to her back: 'There wasn't any blood, was there? I didn't see any blood.'

'No blood,' said Alfreda. 'Not that I looked.'

The two of them lived in a rented flat close to the St Luke's

Theatre complex of which the Pinero Theatre was now the biggest part, although the new, tiny Festival Theatre which was used for student and experimental production was getting increasingly important. Barnabas hoped he might be given a job there if he did well as junior assistant stage manager, than which there was no lower form of life.

Once launched, he meant to move into a place of his own. He loved Alfreda, but she was bossy and inhibiting. A chap found it difficult to maintain his own life.

He loved her though, and protected her.

'May Renier is a bit of a cow, isn't she?' he said as he followed his mother into her office. 'Pooh, the stink in here, you've been smoking.'

'I've got to have one vice.'

'You've got more than one.' He threw open a window. 'I saw May being downright cruel to old Albie . . . and I've seen her with other oldies. She doesn't like them. She's a shoot-all-the-over-fifties sort.'

'She's nearly forty herself,' said Alfreda with a yawn. 'I remember her years ago, both locals, we went to the same infant school, but I don't think she's noticed. No, she's no chicken, and I don't think she likes me very much.'

Barney gave a hoot of laughter. 'Let's shoot her then, shall we?'

'Not till we've got over this production.' Another yawn. 'I wish I could get off to bed.'

'I'll make you a milky drink.'

'Put some whisky in it.'

'Will do.' And he bustled off towards the kitchen area attached to her office. He was a good cook, better than Alfreda, and did most of the housekeeping at home, as a result of which his hands bore numerous cuts and scars. While the milk was heating, he did a small amount of washing up. He was good at it, at home they had a dishwasher but he liked to do some things like knives and silver by hand. He hated mess and there was no denying that Alfreda was careless about her home.

*　　*　　*

Behind them the bodies were being moved on to pallets to take them to the university hospital mortuary where they would be examined.

Two tiny spots of blood were left behind where they had rested.

The Chief Commander and Stella, together with Harry Trent, went home across the courtyard together. Stella went between the two men, arm in arm with both. It was not her usual way of going on, but somehow it seemed right tonight. She was picking up tensions in both that she did not understand.

'Come up for a drink, Harry?'

He shook his head. 'Won't, if you don't mind.'

'Tired myself.'

Another of her smiles, but he was new to them, so he was the more pierced, a kiss on his cheek, a breath of Jolie Madame, and they were gone into their tower.

Coffin had never said a word.

Harry Trent remained outside for a moment, reflecting how like Coffin to end up living in a tower. It fitted with his character somehow, he was a climber.

Harry moved towards his own borrowed front door and took out his key. It was a big old key which looked as though it had been around a long time, perhaps a key from the old church.

He was just fitting it in the door when a figure came out of the shadows.

'Hello, Harry boy, heard you were looking for me.'

Harry moved his head slowly. 'Merry, my God, it's you.'

'Of course. You knew it was me, you knew I'd be here.'

'I did not.'

'Thought it likely, then.'

'How did you know where I would be?'

'Telepathy.' Merry laughed. 'No, a copper told me, he picked it up about the Chief Commander; your friend, I believe. They gossip about him, you know? Well, wouldn't you? I'm on better terms with the coppers than you think. They aren't all trying to run me in, you know.'

'Where are you living?'

'You know: Shambles Passage, old Mother Arbatt's den, and a right old pigsty too, I'm not there more than I can help. Nice place you've got here.'

'Just lent.'

'Like you to ease yourself into somewhere good.'

'You really do think I'm a skunk, don't you?'

'Bit of the pot calling the kettle black, isn't it?' Merry was almost laughing.

Harry took a deep breath. 'Come up and have a drink. I'm glad to see you looking so well. I came here to find you, heard you were here.'

'I don't drink. You're the drinker out of the two of us.'

Since this was true, Harry said nothing, but opened the door. 'Just come in and tell me what you want and what you are doing here.'

Merry did not follow him in, but stayed in the shadows. 'I told you: I heard you were looking for me. We are twins, after all. We keep in touch whether we like it or not.'

'What are you doing in Swinehouse?'

'Earning a living. Just like you. I've got a job in a haulage business. I have to live . . . There's someone else we both know in Spinnergate.'

'I don't want to talk about her. Forget it. I saw you on the TV news, in the street fighting.'

'I wasn't doing any fighting, I was there, yes. You might have been yourself, we were expressing what we felt. I knew that kid, thank God she isn't dead.'

'That's the latest news of her, is it?'

'It is. I went to the hospital myself: stable.'

'Two people died in the theatre tonight.' Harry sounded weary. 'Looks like suicide.'

'I know, I was there, dropped in for the performance, got a cheap ticket. I knew something was up, didn't know what.'

Harry said wearily, 'Look, I don't want to talk about it now, but I want you to remember that I am your twin and I love you and you can talk to me.'

'I know what you think of me: I didn't rape and strangle that girl in North Woolwich, although by God, she nearly raped me. Anyway, she isn't dead. I saw her walking in Greenwich Park the other day.'

That's you all over, Merry, thought Harry. Always with an answer. So glib.

'I won't take a drink off you, but I'll keep in touch, you know where I am.'

Harry nodded. 'So I do. Don't move away without telling me.'

'What about you? Will you push off now you have found me?'

'Not until I have found out what happened to the Macintoshes.'

'Always the detective . . . they were a gloomy old pair, don't wonder they decided to drop over the side. Surprised they did it together, though, never felt they were that keen on each other.'

'They were kind to us.'

'Think so? Didn't feel like kindness to me . . . to tell the truth, I thought they were a spooky couple. I don't feel sorry they are gone.'

'I shouldn't say that aloud too often.'

Merry smiled. 'Don't worry about me, if there's one thing I am good at it is hiding my feelings. Hiding, in fact. It's kind of an occupation.' He looked his brother in the face. 'And that is not a joke, with a childhood like ours, you can't be surprised. I hide, you search, that's your occupation. Two sides of one coin.'

'Oh, shut up.'

'I'll oblige . . . this is me saying goodbye . . . Say goodbye to Lou for me. How is she?'

Harry did not answer, but waved his brother off as the darkness ate him up, they were twins after all and Merry didn't always say what he meant or tell the truth, they couldn't be parted. Or not without surgery.

He was laughing to himself as he went into his borrowed home. 'Might come to that,' he said to himself. 'Oh God, so it might. Take a sharp knife and cut someone out. Hara-kiri of the soul. God, I must be drunker than I thought.'

He picked up the telephone and although it was late, he

41

rang his own home. 'Lou, I'll have to stay on a bit longer
. . . things have happened that mean I must be around. No,
just a continuing investigation.'

He had not told her that he was hunting for Merry, it was
a name he preferred to leave unspoken, a bad word between
them. He had the horrible feeling she liked Merry the better
of the two of them and would have wished to have been his
wife.

He had another drink while he thought about the dead
couple, the Macintoshes. In the morning, if he was still there,
and you never knew, he would talk to John Coffin.

He took a drink to bed, head against the pillows while he
sipped it. Merry was right, Harry was the drinking twin. As
he drank, he thought about his Louise. She was so tall and
slender and desirable. Clever, too.

He finished the drink, put the glass on the floor beside the
bed, wondered briefly what high sexual jinks the bed had
known when Stella had used it, he did not underrate the
Chief Commander.

Enjoying his mildly lascivious thoughts, envious ones too,
he slipped into sleep.

Tomorrow would come whether you like it or not; he
might hide, like Merry, but he could not run away. Things
would have to be said.

Stella took a shower, washing off the scent of Jolie Madame
and replacing it with fresh verbena. Then she knotted the
towelling robe and emerged to confront Coffin.

'Come on, what's up?'

He was standing by the bedroom window, holding the cat,
and staring into the night. Neither seemed happy.

'What do you mean?'

'You were dead silent on the way over from the theatre,
and didn't say a word to Harry. Bit rude, I thought.'

'I'm worried.'

'What about?'

He could have said: the trouble on the streets, the child in
hospital who may be lamed, your man in Rome, and my
own personal little worry, but he said: 'When I touched the

back of the chair where the man Joe Macintosh had been lying, my hand came away with blood on it.'

'Oh.' Stella absorbed this news. 'What does it mean?'

'I don't know, not yet. Maybe nothing. He may have cut himself.'

'Is that all?'

'Harry was odd.'

'He was upset. He knew them, after all.'

'That's what worries me.'

'You can't think he had anything to do with it . . . he was with us all the time.'

'Not *all* the time,' said Coffin in a careful voice, not meeting her eyes as he put Tiddles down on the floor.

'Besides, it was suicide, there was a note.'

'So there was,' said Coffin. 'I noticed.'

Stella leaned back against her pillows. 'Oh, come on, come to bed. You'll feel better in the morning.' She held out her arm. 'Dearest, I know you are full of worry, let me help.'

He sat on the bed beside her. 'Tell me about Jack in Rome?'

Stella opened her eyes wide, then laughed. 'Oh, come on, you aren't thinking anything . . . No, you couldn't. We were acting together.'

'But he keeps telephoning.'

Stella allowed herself a luxurious pause. 'Perhaps he had a little thing about me. Doesn't mean I had one back.'

Coffin groaned. 'Oh, Stella, Stella, Stella.'

'Perhaps a tiny, tiny one, but nothing to count. Truly, am I a liar?'

'I know what you are,' he said slowly. 'A tease.'

She leaned forward and took his hand in a firm grasp. 'But never with you, never with you.' Or this time round, she told herself. I was a devil in the past and punished both of us, but you were no angel either. 'We are truly married, my dear, and I would never risk breaking that bond.'

'I believe.'

One worry gone. Only three to play for now.

DS Davis and DC Armitage had finished their survey of the death site in the theatre, the SOCO had observed and made

43

notes, photographs had been taken, and the two detectives drove back to their Swinehouse office. They were not luxuriously housed, but the canteen was clean and efficient so they went there for a late cup of tea. Davis could always eat, so he had toast as well, while Pat Armitage drank her tea and wished that smoking was not forbidden almost everywhere.

'See you upstairs,' she said, picking up her cup. In the office she could smoke if she was careful about it.

While she drank the tea and gave a grateful draw on the cigarette, she studied the notes and photographs which were already on her desk. She would say one thing for their current SOCO, he was speedy. He would soon move on, SOCOs did if they were good. She had done the job herself for a spell and not found it life enhancing.

She studied the photographs with care, it paid. All right, this was a suicide, they had the note which said so, but the postmortem was still to be done, and anyway, the Chief Commander was involved. So take care, Pat, she thought.

Davis returned as she spread the photographs out on the desk. 'You smell of smoke.'

'You smell of toast.' She had her elbows on the desk and was leaning over the pictures. 'You know, you are quite right, the man does look surprised.' She raised her head. 'I suppose the moment of death can be a surprise even when you have planned it.'

'We don't know that he planned it, maybe she did and didn't tell him.'

Pat Armitage picked up the suicide note, now a neat plastic envelope. The coroner would want to see it. 'It's signed by him. JM.'

'They both had the same initials.'

'True, but I don't think a woman would do it that way.'

The note said: IT IS BEST TO END IT AND GO NOW.

'Bit bleak,' said Davis.

'Probably the best way to do it if you must.'

'That's it, isn't it? If you must. Can't imagine doing it myself.' She stared at the note, which was on yellowing paper, none too clean. 'Maybe she didn't want to.'

'Well, we will never know.'

'I take it you don't believe in the after life?'

'Some of the bodies I have seen, then I hope not. I would definitely not want to know *them* again.'

Then he came out with the great question that no one had so far voiced: 'Why on earth did they do it in a theatre?'

The hospital which housed the mortuary where the two bodies lay was associated with the very new University of Swinehouse, making the third in the Second City. The university had previously been Swinehouse Polytechnic until recent reforms had upped its status, and was housed in the old buildings. The hospital was not new either and the mortuary itself was old, but the new buildings to house the medical school were almost complete. Mr Garden worked in the mortuary but had a fine new office.

Time conscious as he was, Mr Garden got on with things, he was a quick worker. Apart from being what he was, an egoist of the first class, he had no irritating tricks as he worked: he did not hum, nor did he crack foul jokes – the general opinion was he knew no jokes, obscene or otherwise. But he was very interested in the human body, which he admired. If his detractors had realized this, they might have liked him better.

He dealt with Joe's body first, and then Josie's. His face was not one which allowed much expression, but he pursed his lips and raised an eyebrow as he took it all in.

'Well, I never,' he said. 'Interesting.'

He removed his overall and gloves, washed, then went into his office. His secretary, Alma Flint, who had been taking notes, had once worked in Coffin's office, which he felt made a link with the Chief Commander. He found him attractive but tried not to make it too obvious. A little touch of the obvious was not a bad idea, the most surprising people responded on occasion, but one did not stick one's neck out.

He looked at the clock, a pretty little ormolu thing he had picked up at an auction. Nine o'clock, he had started early, having a midday lecture to undergraduates to give. 'Bring me some coffee, Alma.'

The carpet beneath his feet was a rich confection of colour

45

made for him in Portugal. On the wall was an oil painting he had done himself. Coffin had never been here. Yes, he should see it.

'Alma,' he said, as he poured the coffee from the thin china pot. 'Get the Chief Commander on the line. I want to see if he could come round here. It's about the PM on the couple found dead in his wife's theatre.' He liked Stella too, but no bedding *her*!

Coffin had been at work for a couple of hours, engaged in routine administration, when the call came through. His secretary filtered calls as a rule with a fine discrimination, but she let this one through.

'Have you got time to come round? It's walking distance. But quicker if you drive, of course.' This was Garden's notion of a joke. 'Drink before lunch. Have a light lunch, I can lay it on. I thought you might like the PM report in person.'

'Can't you fax it?' Somehow I never like the idea of a meal in a mortuary.

'In my room in the new wing, of course,' said Garden as if he read his thoughts. 'I think you will find this one interesting. And bring that nice Inspector Trent with you. Did I get the name right?'

'You did,' said Coffin without emphasis, but he took in the interest. 'But I am not sure if I know where he is at the moment.'

In fact, he knew very well; Stella had called in on her way to an audition to ask Harry if he wanted anything, there wasn't much food in the flat – and reported that he was stretched out on the bed, dead asleep, with a whisky bottle on the floor beside him. 'But it wasn't quite empty,' she had reported with careful honesty.

'I don't know what to make of him,' Coffin had said, and Stella had replied: 'Why don't you find out?'

'I might ring Greenwich and ask, I still know a few people there.' Even though the old friends had gone, dead or retired. This one of cancer, this one gone to live in Spain. What do old coppers do, he asked himself, they don't retire, they just disappear.

He must have repeated that he was 'Not sure' because he heard Garden say: 'Oh, what a shame. I thought you were friends.'

'We worked together once. It was a long time ago.'

'I thought he had such an interest in this case.'

'Where did you pick that up?' The thing was not to react to Garden, but he could not always manage to hold back.

'Oh, I hear things, words get passed on. I thought he knew the old couple.'

'I believe he did, once. A long while ago.'

'I think he would be interested in what I have found.'

There was no denying a kind of sneaky laughter there. It was true what people said of him: a real bastard. Death was not a subject for humour.

'Of course, the report will be going out to the investigating team, but you know yourself, that takes time.'

So it wasn't just a double suicide?

'I'll see what I can do.'

'Fine, lovely, after one, then?'

The conversation was over.

Coffin went to his window to look out at the scene below. It was something he had done often in his years as Chief Commander of the Second City of London, where he was responsible for keeping the Queen's Peace in a stretch of old Docklands. Spinnergate, Swinehouse and East Hythe made up his territory. He had lived in Spinnergate for some years now, ever since he took up his present position; he loved his tower dwelling, it seemed his first real home. Perhaps this was because he shared now with Stella, at last his wife. Close by was the theatre complex created by Stella in the church itself. The old churchyard remained, but was now a pleasant garden with flowers and shrubs around the graves bearing the names of long-dead parishioners: Ducketts, Cruins, Birdways, Deephearts and Earders, families still to bc found on thc school rolls and among the ratepayers of the area. Also among the criminal fraternity, for the Second City had always had its violent side, its inhabitants not easy to control as the Romans and the Normans had found in

47

their day. There was a deeply ingrained Them and Us mentality which Coffin still confronted.

The injured child had been a Birdways, Thelma Birdways of Pomeranian Street, Swinehouse.

It was a name he was not going to forget. Birdways – a good old Anglo-Saxon name imbedded in there, he thought, just as with Earders, but Cruin he felt might be a corruption of an early Celtic name.

They had been there a long time, a lot of the people in his bailiwick, nor had successive waves of invaders and immigrants moved them on.

He liked the view, liked his office, liked having a large staff, it had to be admitted: and liked his position. It was a long way from that earlier basement office of his in Deptford which was reputed to have rats and certainly had mice. Good days, though, in many ways – young, energetic, thrusting days.

Drunker days too, a little voice inside said, that's behind you and you owe that to Stella, so whatever she does now or has done, you owe her.

He turned away from the window. What had to be done, had better be done.

He picked up the telephone. He knew the man in Greenwich CID that he wanted.

'Fergus? Is that you?' But he knew it was, he recognized the gravelly smoker's voice, even if unheard for some years.

Chief Inspector George Ferguson admitted that it was indeed he, and to whom was he speaking.

'Your grammar has improved since the old days . . . you would have said who were you speaking to once.'

There was a silence, and then, 'Coffin, by God, haven't they knighted you?'

'Not done the actual deed. Coming up soon. I'm a kind of honorary knight at the moment . . . but as they say: it comes up with the rations. How are you?'

'I'm fine. Looking forward to my retirement.'

'Don't say it.'

'Oh, I've a way to go yet. I only said I was looking forward to it. So would you round here.'

'Bad, is it?'

'Well, it doesn't get any better.'

All that said, Ferguson sounded cheerful enough. 'So what can I do for you? I take it there is something?'

'Harry Trent is one of yours, isn't he?'

There was a pause. 'What's Harry done?'

'Nothing, nothing,' said Coffin hastily. 'He's visiting, that's all.'

Another pause, then Ferguson spoke, his voice seeming to be relieved rather than otherwise. 'That's where he went? He has been having a spot of sick leave.'

'Oh? Why?'

'A villain stuck a knife into him . . . could have done for him, but mercifully he got away with it lightly, it was a shock, though.'

'Would be. Well, thanks for telling me. Did he say anything about his brother?'

'Didn't know he had one. But he didn't talk about himself much . . . although I have heard' – he kept his voice cool and careful – 'that things were not going all that well with his wife. Just a canard, I expect.'

'Thanks for telling me.'

'What is this about his brother?'

'I'm not sure.' He may not have one . . . 'Forget this conversation for a bit, will you? I will come back to you.'

Then for a little while they talked over other things: the new instructions for the police from the Home Office, the debate about carrying arms, and trouble on the streets.

This conversation had been conducted on his special private line which Coffin used again to telephone Stella's old number which presumably Harry Trent would answer.

No answer.

He had a choice, he could leave Harry alone to whatever he was up to, if anything, and go round to see this 'interesting' postmortem report on his own, or he could go and bang on the door himself.

He had a key, but he would probably not use it.

He rang the bell once, and within a second, the door was opened by Harry who looked neat, well shaved and tidy, with only a heaviness around the eyes to suggest the picture Stella had painted. Coffin decided not to mention her visit to collect any message or post which might have arrived from the surprising number of people who still thought she lived there. Including, he sometimes thought, Stella herself. He was not a bit surprised that she had slipped in this morning. Curiosity on several counts, he guessed.

'You are invited to a drink with Dennis Garden to talk over his postmortem report, he thinks it might be interesting.' He added: 'I ought to warn you that I think he might be interested in you.'

Harry grinned, which made his face look younger and happier. 'Don't worry. I can handle that. No problem. Yes, I'd like to hear what he's found.' The smile left his face, ageing him by ten years at once. 'I'm coming.'

'Do you know,' he said, as they drove towards the Swinehouse university building. 'I had a dream that Stella came in and looked down at me while I was asleep.'

Coffin did not answer, but as he drove he had a picture of his Stella, horizontal, with the hint of wings, floating in the air above Harry Trent.

As Dennis Garden poured out the drinks he accepted their praise of the pleasantness of his room. 'You know, when I started out all those dread years ago, I worked in a hovel, a positive slum, in an old workhouse. Damp ran down the walls and one was never far from a rat, but still I was expected to perform. I was assistant to old Jason then.'

He looked at Coffin as he handed him his drink. He hadn't asked what either wanted but assessed them both as gin-with-tonic-and-ice drinkers, policemen often were if they could get it. It was entirely in character with him that he should do this.

'I remember him,' said Coffin.

'Terrible death he had.' A touch of professional relish in Garden's voice. 'Burnt. Spontaneous combustion, we thought, but it turned out he did it himself with a lighted cigarette and too much whisky.'

On the table were plates of smoked salmon sandwiches –

and not from Max's, Coffin assessed, made them himself probably, he was said to be handy in the kitchen. Neat-fingered, well, in his trade he would have to be.

Garden sipped his drink and then spoke: 'The reason I got you here is . . .' He paused. 'It was not suicide. It's murder.' He added: 'In both cases.'

'I thought it would be something like that you had to say.' So what about that curious note, suggesting suicide?

'I knew you'd guess. I'll say this for you, Coffin, you are never slow on the uptake. You're quick.'

'Too quick sometimes.'

'That too,' accepted Garden. 'Yes, there is a small but deep puncture at the base of the skull. Just where the neck joins. Neat job.'

Harry Trent put his drink down, banged it on the table. 'I'd like to see the two bodies.'

'Not now, not before we've finished our drinks and had a sandwich.'

'I would like to see them.'

'Perhaps it would be best to get it over,' said Coffin.

Garden sighed, but nodded. 'OK, OK, follow me.' He led the way out of his room, into the lift, then along another corridor which seemed to slide, imperceptibly, to earlier years, back in time, back into another century.

Coffin brushed against one wall as they walked and the dust of past years came off on his jacket. I won't have to live so much longer to live into another century, he told himself, but this wall belongs to the century before that.

Garden pushed through several swing doors. 'You can't eat in here, you know. Not allowed. A lab like this is not the place to eat or drink.'

'I wasn't thinking of doing so.'

'There's the university dining room but the food is poor. That's why I bring stuff from home.' Garden pushed through the last door into frigid antisepsis.

He went over to a table. 'This one and the next,' he nodded.

Harry went over and drew back the sheet that covered one face, then moved on to the next. Coffin watched in silence.

'These are not the Macintoshes, not the ones I knew. They are not the right people.'

Coffin turned to look at Garden whose eyes were bright. 'So what else?' He could tell the man was vibrant with repressed emotion; he was enjoying his moment.

'I'll tell you what else: they are not a man and a woman. Both men.'

When the news gets around, as inevitably it does, Hyde begins to froth inside. He knows that he must have been out again in the world, something he is never quite sure about. He becomes excited, as if he had somehow inhaled the essences of Joe and Josie like a druggie cigarette.

3

Coffin and Harry Trent walked away together to where Coffin's car was parked by a side wall of the university block. No one had eaten the sandwiches, unless Garden had gone back for a quick snack. Coffin thought this likely on what he knew of him. He could feel his own thoughts rumbling inside him like indigestion: I don't like that man, he thinks he's God because he deals in the dead.

Just as they got to the car Harry stopped, he put his hand on the car bonnet, then staggered back to lean on the wall. He was pale and sweating. 'I'm going to be sick.'

Coffin took his arm. 'If you mean that, come this way . . . there's a gutter here.' Too much whisky last night, and too much emotion now. He wondered about the emotions.

He felt angry rather than sympathetic. People ought to manage themselves better. He had wanted to question Harry about the Macintoshes. It looked as though there were certainly going to be questions asked.

He moved back towards the car, meaning to keep out of the way, only to be turned back by the sound of Harry retching and choking. Sympathetic in spite of himself, he handed the man a large white clean handkerchief.

'Thanks,' muttered Harry. 'Sorry.'

'Don't worry.'

'Wash it, give it you back,' came through the muffling linen.

'Don't bother,' said Coffin hastily. 'Put it in that bin over there . . . when you are ready.' He moved away again, not looking. Better and kinder not to look at a man in that state. But questions he would ask.

After a second sneaking look, he decided that Harry was not going to die on him so he went to sit in the car. Presently, he felt Harry crawl into the seat beside him.

'Sorry . . . do I stink?'

'Nothing much,' said Coffin, winding down the window. 'There's a shower in my bathroom next to my office. Have one when we get back. I want to speak to you, anyway.'

The Chief Commander's new secretary was not in the room when they got back, nor was there any sign of his assistant who had a small room, nothing more than a cubby hole with a window, off the main office. He had discovered to his sadness that there was a rapid turnover in his staff, always, it seemed, for good and natural reasons like impending childbirth or the transfer of a spouse, so that Sylvia and Gillian who now worked for him as secretaries, taking shifts so that one was always on duty, were not the same young women as six months ago, and might change again in another six months. He accepted but lamented: he liked to get used to people and to work with them.

His assistant, Paul Masters, was a career officer, it was that sort of appointment, so he did not expect him to stay, he would make a move.

There had been a turnout of the upper echelons of the CID and uniformed branch in the last year, some of which departures he had engineered, but he still had his old friend Archie Young, now a chief superintendent, a rank which might soon go.

Coffin started to think about his current life as if he was outside it all, Coffin watching.

Coffin has Archie Young on his side – they do pick sides, it's like a tough school game or a jungle fight, of all this Coffin is thinking. Archie is definitely his.

But Archie is on six months' leave with his clever, ambitious wife who has left the police service for a post in a Midlands university, taking Archie with her if she can, so Archie too may be lost to him.

He still has Phoebe Astley, of course, but she is deeply occupied with her Special (S) Unit which she had been brought in to run, and so they only meet on formal occasions which for many reasons, not unconnected with their past, suits them both.

So Coffin has to make do with Superintendent Phil Lewinder whom he is not sure if he likes. He comes back to the present because he hears movement from the bathroom.

At the moment, a drink would be appreciated, strong and cold, but not in front of Harry Trent. He had no very strong reasons to believe that the man had a drink problem, but he knew signs. He had been down that road himself once.

'Sorry. Can't apologize enough.' Harry reappeared, hair wet and sleeked down. Coffin had to admit he was a good-looking man. For some reason, or one he would be ashamed to admit, this irritated him. 'I don't know why that happened.'

'Too much whisky last night?'

There was a moment of silence. 'So Stella was not a dream but real.'

It was Coffin's time to look abashed. 'She forgot you were there, went in to collect her post and messages; she uses the place as a kind of office.'

'Well, I must have looked a sight and I don't blame her for saying so . . . The truth . . .' He paused.

Perhaps he doesn't know what the truth is, thought Coffin.

'The truth is I was upset at what happened last night. Somehow anything to do with the Macs goes right inside me and out the other side like a knife . . .' He paused again. 'Oh God, I suppose that's what happened to them? A knife went in and out.' He showed signs of nausea again.

'Except it wasn't them,' said Coffin, handing him a glass of water. 'The ones we knew as the Macintoshes, the ones who sold hamburgers and hot dogs, but not your Macintoshes. Are you sure about that, by the way?'

Harry drained the glass. 'Last night, I was sure at first, at that first look, and didn't know what to make of it, then when everything was going on, I thought: well, I was only a kid when I last saw them, nine or ten, perhaps I am wrong . . . They could have changed. It's been a long while, people do change.'

'Aged. We all do,' said Coffin.

'They hadn't aged though, younger if anything and different. I realized all that when I was back in the flat.'

'How long were you with them?'

'About six months, the pair of us.'

'Did you like them?'

'Hated their guts.'

Coffin took the glass. 'Somehow I got the feeling you did, that got across. Let's have some coffee. Gillian (or it might be Sylvia) always leaves some ready.' He went across to the coffee machine, poured two cups. 'We'll all have caffeine poisoning in this place one day.' He handed across a cup. 'Smoke if you like, I don't but I haven't declared the room a non-smoking zone. Why did you dislike them?'

'They were tough with us. Rules and judgement . . . not physically unkind, although they did whack us a bit, but mentally . . . Yes.' He gulped some coffee down.

'What about your brother? Did he dislike them too?'

Harry looked down at his cup. His voice when he spoke was sad. 'Yes. But there was a difference, he wanted to love them. I never did. So it was worse for him when he had to hate them.'

Coffin considered. 'Come on, Harry, there has to be a bit more, why did he have to hate them?'

'He had a kitten, a little stray he found, he was feeding it . . . they drowned it, they made him watch. A punishment because he had lied about taking bits of food.'

Stinkers, Coffin thought, they were clearly not the Joe and Josie Macintosh he knew, but a couple with iron inside them. 'Did you watch it too?'

Harry Trent frowned. 'You know, I am not quite sure if I did. I feel as though I saw it . . . but perhaps it was the other one. You know what twins are like: what does for one, does for the other.'

'If you say so.'

'I still felt bad when I saw those two. Who are they?'

'That's the question.'

Coffin was pacing up and down the room as he often did when he was thinking. Stella said it made her dizzy.

'So what have we got: a murder accompanied by a suicide

note . . . that is one problem. A married couple who turned out to be not man and wife but two men . . . all right, I accept that. But this couple are not the ones you knew under that name.' He was up to the window now and turning back. 'Now that's odd.'

Harry kept quiet.

'Are you sure that they are not the pair you knew?'

'I don't know I'd go into the witness box, or how I would stand up to questioning on it,' he said with a slight smile, 'but inside myself, yes, I'm sure.'

'Think about it.'

'I am, all the time . . . I'll say something,' he came up with suddenly. 'My Mrs Macintosh was a woman . . . I know she was.'

'Saw her undressed, did you?'

'No, never, of course not − a pair of puritans like that, I expect they undressed in the dark, how they ever brought themselves to have sex, I don't know . . . maybe never . . . except there was a daughter . . . But Mrs Mac was a woman, all right.'

'So how do you know?'

'I smelt her . . . she had a woman's smell.'

Coffin was silenced but interested, the remark shed a light on eight-year-old Harry, he thought.

He looked down at his hands, broad, tough, working hands, but with well-shaped nails. 'When we get more information about the likely weapon, we will be a step ahead. Something smallish in diameter and sharp.'

'A chisel, sharpened at home?' suggested Trent.

'Could be. Something more high-grade, I think.'

'What about something being used in the current production? A bayonet from *Journey's End*?'

'I think they blunt them, but they're roughly the right size for the wound . . . might have been sharpened and used.' He frowned. 'Worth a thought. But I am sure that Lewinder has considered it, he's a methodical fellow . . . Motive, now: why were they killed? Well, when we know more about them, then the motive will probably appear. Who are they? That's a big question.'

'But not the only one, is it?'

'No, indeed. Why did they take over the identity of two other people, and how did they manage it?'

'If they were a married pair of homosexuals, then that might have been the reason, or part of it. It could have suited them.'

'Yes, that must come into it.' Coffin considered. 'Yes, I have seen them together, and whatever their relationship, they were happy in it. They liked each other.'

'And where are my Macintoshes? And why was their name adopted?'

Coffin shrugged. 'That's two questions, isn't it? You knew them. In your opinion, would they have cleared out? And why was their name passed on? Maybe they sold it for trading.' It seemed to have been accepted as such by the neighbourhood which had been unworried and unquestioning. Didn't care.

Harry looked troubled, doubtful. 'They were very possessive of what they owned. But yes, I suppose so, if they were in trouble and wanted out.'

'Like ill-treating a child?'

'I think they would have braved anything out if they could, but it would depend, if the child died . . . Yes, then they might clear out and get this other pair to cover for them.

'But –' Harry began, then stopped. 'I'm thinking this through and I'm not sure what I am seeing.'

'Let me help: the dead pair must have known what happened to the couple whose identities they took over.'

'You think so?'

'Inescapable.' Once again, he paused to think. 'Let me correct that: they may not have known exactly where and how the Macintoshes went. No, we can't assume too much about what they knew and didn't know.'

'They may not have wanted to know.'

Coffin nodded. 'Yes, I agree, it may have suited them to take over new names without wanting to look too close. They may have been paid.'

'Be lucky to get anything out of the Macs I knew unless they were in bad trouble.'

'I think they may have been,' said Coffin in a sober voice. 'But there's something else to think about: we have two murdered people, the substitute Macintoshes are dead. It means that out there, is a person probably violent and certainly dangerous. Motive there to be discovered.'

A tiger walking through the day and night.

'I don't see this as a random or purposeless killing . . . no, it looks planned to the last detail to me . . .'

'Yes,' said Harry. 'I discovered myself that tickets had been sent to them . . . Max said so.' He said slowly: 'I'm trying not to think about Merry.'

'You brought his name in yourself,' Coffin reminded him.

'So I did.' He took a deep breath to stop a wave of nausea sweeping over him. 'I shall go on looking for him. I suppose your lot will be as well?'

Coffin did not answer directly. 'There's one other big puzzle: the suicide letter. Where does that fit in? It was a lie and a silly lie, because the fact it was murder not suicide was bound to be discovered. So why was it there?'

'A joke?'

'I doubt it, I don't see this killer as a joker, do you?'

Heavily, Harry said: 'No.'

'Well, there we are, that's our problem and I expect Phil Lewinder who thought it could be nicely tidied away as an eccentric suicide is already tearing his hair out.'

'He hasn't got much, if he's the one I saw.'

It was true that Superintendent Lewinder had gone prematurely bald.

'So what will you do?' Coffin asked Harry Trent.

'I'll stay around, you said so anyway, but I won't hang on in Stella's place – it was kind of her to let me perch there. I'll find somewhere else.'

Coffin knew that he was right to distance himself from Harry Trent now the investigation of the double deaths was murder.

'Might be best. Let me know if I can help.'

It was a dismissal, as Harry recognized wryly to himself. I know my place, he told himself. I am on the outer edge.

It was not unknown territory to him, one way and another

he had been there before. As a detective it had been an advantage to feel he knew the lower depths, he could move naturally in certain circles. He had even advanced his career by doing undercover work. I was a kind of rat, he thought, moving about in the debris and the dirt. He wondered if Coffin knew about that work . . . But of course, he would find out, he trusted the man's professional expertise.

Harry went back to Stella's apartment where he packed his few possessions. He had made no impact on it and he left it tidy. An opened window had blown away his only legacy: the smell of whisky.

He left his bags in the hall, ready to be collected when he had a base.

Before he went, he telephoned his wife, he would pay Stella for the call.

There was no answer, only Louise's voice, telling him she was not there and to leave his name and a message and she would get back to him.

'Lou? Where are you? I have tried a couple of times to get you and you aren't there. Or are you there and not answering? Lou, don't do this to me.'

She was beautiful, his Louise, and clever, way out of his class, he knew that; she was too good for him. Or he was too bad for her, he never knew which way round to put it.

The Chief Commander might have had something of the same problem with his own wife, but it appeared to be a problem he had surmounted. Only you never knew. People had a public face and a private face, and police as much as anyone. Perhaps more so. The trouble with the police job was that you had to be two people.

He wished now that he had not embarked on this search for Merry (Louise had never encouraged it, rather the reverse), and that he had not got in touch with John Coffin.

'Was all that talk in his office for his benefit or directed at me?' he asked himself. 'And if so, what was he telling me?' Nothing good. In spite of the drinks earlier, he was thirsty.

Wrapping both personae up in one, remembering that as a twin there was a bit of Merry in him as well as something of himself in Merry, he took himself off to Max's eating place round the corner, which was both cosy and stylish. The place at this time, always popular, was beginning to fill up with people coming in for tea or just a drink and a cup of coffee. There was a public telephone at the end of the room. He looked at it wistfully, debating another try to talk to his wife; he took one step forward before changing his mind.

But his progress had brought him up to a table where two people were sitting. He knew the faces. Alfreda.

Alfreda looked at him doubtfully, then decided to smile. Her son, sitting hunched over his cup of coffee, did not.

'Join us,' said Alfreda, deciding Harry was both tired and harmless. 'We will be quiet. You be quiet and I will be quiet. Know what I mean?'

'Well . . .' Harry looked at Barnabas who glowered back.

'Take no notice of Barnabas, he's in a bad mood. Two heads, he's got sometimes.' She stretched out a hand.

Harry nodded and sat down. 'Thanks, Alfreda, Barnabas.'

'Call me Barney.' But he managed to make it not friendly.

'I saw you last night . . . we almost met last night.'

'We certainly did . . . if you can call it meeting. What a business. It made me feel ill. I feel ill now.' There were dark shadows under her eyes. 'So you're a policeman.'

'Not on the case. Just visiting. Not digging up anything.'

'Better not.' The waiter came forward and Harry ordered. 'Coffee and a sandwich . . . ham, I think, and maybe a cheese as well.' Suddenly he felt very hungry.

'Ah.' Alfreda sounded almost disappointed. It struck Harry that she had been hoping to find out details about the case.

'You staying with our lady boss?' Her tone suggested admiration but not overmuch love for Stella Pinero.

'No.' The coffee had arrived, hot and strong. 'No, Stella was kind enough to let me have a bed for a while, but I'm looking for somewhere else for a few days. Got business here.'

Alfreda stirred some sugar into her coffee, the sun on her reddish mane of hair, she was a lovely sight, as Harry took in. 'I could let you have a room for a few days . . . My lodger, she was my assistant, a student really, on work training, got a permanent job in Sheffield, and left suddenly. They do, these kids, but I'm glad she got a job.'

'Bradford,' muttered Barney.

'All right, Bradford, but it's a job – you'll find out yourself soon.' She turned to Harry. 'I don't know how you'd feel about it. Just temporary, of course . . .' They eyed each other cautiously. Spinnergate made you that way. There was too much history in Spinnergate.

'I will only want it for a short time. I'll pay, of course.'

'To be honest, I'll be glad of the money, the theatre doesn't make you rich. Right, bring your things around . . . Alloa Road, just round the back of St Luke's. Barney will give you a hand.' She looked at her son. 'Don't be put off by that scowl, he's a nice boy really. At least I think he is.'

The boy smiled, an unexpectedly charming smile. 'Take no notice of my mother, she doesn't know half.'

Harry said seriously: 'Do you prefer to be Barnabas or Barney?'

The reply was equally serious. 'Sometimes one, sometimes the other, it's a mood thing, if you can understand.'

'I absolutely can,' said Harry.

Coffin returned to his routine, mundane work, dealt with it efficiently and swiftly, then he went for a walk.

Not for nothing was the Chief Commander's code name WALKER. When the word went out on the airwaves that WALKER was on the move, then the constable on the beat, and the men in the patrol car, were on alert. It paid.

But before he went walking, Coffin spoke on the telephone to his wife.

'I've seen Harry, he's moving out.'

'I didn't mind him.' Stella's voice was mild, she liked Harry, she thought.

'I prefer it.'

'He's your chum, but if you say so . . .'

'I do. He's better out.'

'All right then, he's out.'

'Thank you, love.'

Stella laughed, she was not amenable to blandishment,

which she recognized when she heard it. 'He's up to something,' she said aloud to the empty room.

She had been on the telephone to her agent who had an offer: New York was on the cards, Philadelphia and Boston to follow. She was considering it all, a long time away from a marriage that might need looking after. Coffin had been odd lately. Not unloving, just different.

She heard her front door open and Harry and Barney come in to collect his luggage. So she knew he was moving into Alloa Road with Alfreda Boxer. Stella smiled; I hope he realizes what a maneater she is.

Coffin strode through the streets, walking fast and confidently, he crossed a busy main road, turned left, then left again, and this brought him to an area of large, plain buildings which sat heavily on the ground. Twelve floors high and lined with walkways, bleak but well lit at all hours. There were four such blocks set up one after the other like the toys of a careful giant. Then beyond, with a small open space between, were another four blocks. There was a neat unpleasing symmetry about it all, as if the creator could only think in large even numbers.

In the middle of the open space, heavily oppressed by its massive neighbours, was an old bay-windowed house surrounded by a neglected garden with an old carriage house and a stable behind. Parked in the short driveway was Joe and Josie's van. It had their name on it in large, gold letters.

This, or what was left of it, was Tolliver Street. A strange little oasis left over from another century, another way of life.

A uniformed police officer stood at the front door talking to an elderly man.

As Coffin came closer he saw that the constable was very young indeed with pale blue eyes in a red face, while the man was more than elderly, he was old, a brown wrinkled face with heavy dark spectacles.

As the Chief Commander walked up the path, the old man nodded at the constable and scuttered past Coffin, avoiding his gaze.

The constable saluted, he recognized this man.

'Who was that?'

'A Mr Weldon, sir. Teddy Weldon, actually.'

'You know him?'

'My parents used to live in the flat above where he now lives, sir.'

'What did he want?'

'Just nosey, sir, he likes to know what goes on. He can't see much but there is nothing wrong with his hearing.'

'Is he the only one you've had?' said Coffin with sympathy.

The young man grinned. 'Not likely, sir, about the twentieth. But he's the only one who knew them from way back. Everyone else is sort of new round here.'

'What about you?'

'No, sir, came here with my parents about five years ago . . . came from over the river.'

Over the river, a foreign country.

'Like it here?'

'You get used to it,' said the constable. 'And here we have a decent flat, and over in Deptford . . .' He shrugged.

Coffin nodded. 'I'm going in for a look round.'

The lad, he was no more, stood back to let him pass. 'Yes, sir. Superintendent Lewinder has just left.'

Phil Lewinder, of course. Naturally he would have been in.

'Anyone else?'

'The forensic team was in earlier, sir, I believe, but I wasn't on duty then.'

Forensics, that too was to be expected, and the Chief Commander would expect their report on his desk, but his own thoughts he would keep to himself.

'Did you know the Macintoshes?'

'Not really, sir, apart from the van. I've had a hot dog or an ice-cream, it was good stuff, but that was it . . . they were polite but private.' He nodded sagely, he was pink-cheeked and bright of eye. He looked like a country boy, but no, straight out of deepest Deptford.

I can believe it, Coffin thought, they had a lot to be private about. Without another word, he passed through the door and into the house. It smelt as if no windows had been opened for a long time, it was dark and probably damp.

There were six rooms, three on a floor. He walked through it slowly, taking it in. The top-floor rooms were furnished, but neglected. Three small beds were crammed into one room in the front top and two in the back top, the last room was bare. There was a small bathroom and lavatory. Bars on the windows, linoleum, old at that, on the floor.

Not cosy, he thought, and it bore out Harry Trent's judgement that life with the Macintoshes had not been comfortable. But he had to admit that even after all this time, the top floor looked orderly and clean.

He walked down the stairs where it was clear that Joe and Josie had lived in these rooms; bedroom, living room and kitchen. It was in these rooms he saw traces of the forensic team at work. He had no idea what they had been looking for, and possibly they had little themselves.

Lewinder had sent them in on a trawling trip to flush up what they could. It was what he would have done himself.

There was one big double bed, tidily made up, a dressing table, and two big wall cupboards. The doors were swinging open, one cupboard with a small row of women's clothes, and the other with men's clothes. Who owned and wore which was anyone's guess. Perhaps they were interchangeable.

The kitchen was equally neat, the refrigerator well stocked with food. It was a very big refrigerator because Joe and Josie (he found that he could not call them the Macintoshes any longer, they were Joe and Josie) kept the supplies for the van there.

No sign that the people who lived here had planned suicide. But no sign either that they had expected to be murdered. They might have had some idea, they might have been worried, but that alarm did not write itself on the wall.

In the big living room were two comfortable armchairs, a round table in the window, and a big television set. A bowl of fruit, a vase of flowers, both testified to an expectation of continued life.

It was pleasant enough in these rooms although the

furniture was old and much worn; the sombre atmosphere of the upper rooms which might have held sway down here too, had been exorcized by the other pair.

Coffin stood in the middle of the room. They were a decent pair, he thought sadly. They had their secrets but they left behind them a good feel.

The telephone stood on the table, and he pressed the redial button to hear what he got.

A pause while the number rang out: 'St Luke's Theatre, Box Office,' a voice trilled.

Coffin put the receiver down without answering. It was natural that one of them should have rung the theatre to check after receiving the unexpected tickets.

'You know Mr Weldon,' he said to the constable at the door. 'Is this a good time to call on him?'

'It's always a good time with him. Ground floor in the Armstrong Building, 1B, it's second on the left. You'll get in.'

Coffin understood what the young man meant when he walked through the entrance hall, bleak and smelling of disinfectant with an undersmell less clean.

The door of 1B stood open.

The hall was crowded with furniture: a long sofa against one wall, battered but still comfortable, covered in aged chintz, two chairs on the other wall, and a bookcase, empty of books but full of shoes, bits of china, and a couple of hats.

'Hello? Mr Weldon?'

A thin, old figure wearing a soft woollen cap and a matching jacket – that is, they had matched once but the jacket was stained and torn – appeared at the door end of the hall.

'I'm here.'

'Can we talk?' Coffin introduced himself.

'I know who you are, seen you around.'

Coffin looked at the open door. 'Is it safe to leave the door wide like this?'

Mr Weldon laughed, a robust laugh for one of his age and size. 'No one would come in here, let them just try. I've got my Nelly.' He turned his head. 'Nelly, come here.'

'Ah . . . Nelly?' Coffin expected to see a woman as frail and old as her husband.

A large and shaggy Alsatian dog, yellow of tooth and rakish of eye, appeared round the door. She gave Coffin a measured look.

'She has a lovely growl,' said her proud owner. 'Scare the lights out of you, but she's as gentle as a dove, really.'

Coffin, measuring the teeth, wondered. Some dove.

'So what's this about? I know who you are, remember you from when you were walking the beat.'

'In Greenwich?'

'Yes, I worked on the river. Moved here when my wife died. My second wife.'

'Second, eh?'

'Maisie. She knew you too.'

'Really?'

'Knew your mum.'

Coffin was silenced for a moment. 'More than I did.'

'Oh, you weren't born then, they were at school together. Maryon Park School. I was there myself, but I was only in the babies' class and they were big girls. I married out of my class that time.'

'How many times?'

'Three.' He patted the dog's head. 'But I prefer this bitch to any of them. I'm a registered partially sighted man.'

Coffin studied Nelly as she loped forward. 'Is she a properly trained blind guide dog?' he asked doubtfully.

'Trained by me.' Another grin.

'In other words, she bites those you don't like?'

'Not bite, no, just a little nibble. She's been valuable to me, has Nelly.'

Coffin decided to pass over Nelly, although she still looked far from friendly, with a show of big, yellow teeth.

'Did you ever get confused between Mr Macintosh and his wife?' A question which could have been phrased better, he thought, but it was said now.

'Why are you asking this?' demanded Mr Weldon. 'Think I don't know a man from a woman, even if I am partially sighted.'

Coffin passed over this doubtful statement as there was every evidence he had not noticed anything wrong with Joe and Josie.

'Did you ever buy anything from the stall run by Joe and Josie?'

'No, I don't eat that stuff. I do my own cooking. I still can, ask Nell.'

'But you saw them around?'

'No, my distance vision is poor, and I never felt like going real close.'

Coffin decided to try another way: 'What happened when you were moved out of your original house into here?'

'Didn't happen all at once, not to me, I was in hospital when we were cleared out. They put the blocks of flats up first, some of them, and then moved us, then they knocked down the houses and cleared the ground for more. But I was in hospital, like I said, and my daughter saw to the move. She had Nelly too.'

Nelly looked up at her name in his voice, and went across to lay her head on his knee.

'When I was better I had been moved. Lost all my old neighbours, they seemed to go elsewhere, but I didn't mind.'

'But one house was left standing?'

'Yes, they couldn't get to move that.' He was vague. 'I don't know why. Councils can usually do what they want. I heard they had to wait.'

'And it was empty for a time?'

'I heard it was, but not for long, because the people came back.'

'The same people?'

'They might not have been, there were stories about that, nephew and niece or cousins or something, but it might not have been true. And the neighbours who would have known had gone, they were all old people; I reckon they might be dead by now.'

No, not dead, Coffin thought, just moved away and not bothering their heads. He didn't blame them.

An empty house into which Joe and Josie moved, hiding

their identities behind those of the previous owners who no longer seemed to be around.

He said goodbye to Mr Weldon, risked a quick pat on Nelly's head, she didn't growl but looked surprised, and departed.

He had to decide then whether to go straight back to his own headquarters or make one other call.

He wanted to make the call.

He wanted to see where Merry Trent had lived. It was within walking distance if you were quick. Shambles Passage lay past Brunswick Street and beyond Cowper's Alley and if you did not know it was there you might miss the entrance altogether.

It was a quiet, ancient street which had once been called Brunswick Passage, before the animal slaughterer, long gone in his turn, had moved in and passed on the name of his trade. Grey white lozenge on the bricks where the first name had been painted, probably in 1830 or thereabouts, could be seen, faintly. Once it had been a respectable, prosperous row of houses where the master of a ship, home town London, had lived, or one of the chief men in the great port which London had been, but now it was changed, run down in the world.

Number Two, it also now called itself Percival Lodge, was where Merry Trent had lodged by all accounts, if he could be said to live anywhere. At all events, it was a lodging house and a run-down one at that.

The door was not locked so Coffin pushed it open to walk in. But he did not get far before an elderly figure came out of a door on the dark corridor to confront him. He took it for granted this was a woman since she wore a fur hat, but her legs were covered in solid blue trousers which ended in boots.

'Who are you, and what is your business?' The voice was deep and husky and could have belonged to either sex, but it was an educated voice.

Coffin introduced himself. She came right up and stared in his face. 'Yes, I've seen you around, I recognize you. Mrs Percival.' She held out her hand. Coffin took her hand, which was warm and dry. Also strong, she got a good grip on him. 'What's become of Ma Arbatt?'

'Still around but mostly in bed. I'm her daughter.'

'You're not who I expected,' he said, before he could stop himself.

'What did you expect? Someone like an animal just because it's a cheap lodging? I run it well enough, it's a living.'

'I am interested in one of your lodgers, a man called Trent . . . Merry Trent, he is usually known as.'

'Don't know the name, but we don't bother much about names here.' She looked sharp-eyed, as if she could bother if she chose. 'People tell such lies. Of course, they have to register, but I wouldn't trust to it, and I don't remember that name.'

Coffin produced a photograph, hardly a flattering one, of Harry's brother taken in full shout at the demonstration. Coffin had had it made for him.

'Oh him, yes, he took a room for two weeks, paid in advance, well, I always insist on that, but he hasn't been around for some days.' She held up the photograph. 'Yes, that's him, but not a pretty look.'

'No, he was angry.'

'You can see that. Mind now, he was an angry man but I only saw him once. I think we've lost him.'

She was philosophical, after all, he had paid, it was why he had paid, why they all paid in advance. One 'lost' them sometimes.

'If you ever had him,' Coffin said thoughtfully.

'What does that mean?'

Coffin did not answer, but put another question: 'Anyone here got any idea where he might be?'

She shook her head. 'Shouldn't think so. And they'd never tell you, you being police.'

'Even though I am police, would you tell me?'

She considered. 'I might do.' Again that smile, full of secrets. 'But I don't know. Honest.'

Coffin accepted what she said, although he was sure that Mrs Percival and honesty were far apart.

He said goodbye and walked out into Shambles Passage.

It was quiet and becoming dark; as he walked into Cowper's Alley and turned into Brunswick Street, it was even darker.

There were trees lining the little road, stunted London trees, but heavy with vegetation as autumn drew on. As he stopped, he had the sensation of having been followed. He swung round, nothing to be seen, but a body might have tucked itself behind a tree.

He walked on, but slowly, on the alert. He heard movement behind him and froze, then he turned on his heel.

As he did so, a knife flashed forward towards his ribs. He only knows one spot to strike, this chap, he thought, as he knocked the knife aside. It skimmed his wrist, cutting the flesh, before falling into the gutter.

The figure behind him, with a mask drawn down over the face, skidded away through the trees. Coffin followed, blinded by a tree branch, and when he looked again, the figure had disappeared.

He swore and went back to where he had knocked the knife into the kerb, noticing as he picked it up that there was blood dripping down his wrist.

He bound his wrist up with his handkerchief, and continuing to swear quietly to himself, he walked back out of Cowper's Alley.

The patrol car that tried to keep close when WALKER was on the loose was drawn up by the side of the road.

'There's a joker out there with a knife who tried to attack me. Dressed in black, only he may have changed already. Keep an eye open and bring in anyone suspicious.'

To himself, he thought, they would be lucky if they found his attacker. Nor was he proud of his own part, he should have brought the man in himself.

He made his way to Superintendent Lewinder's office, where the latter was on the telephone.

'I think you should search the house that the Macintosh pair lived in. Pull it to bits if you have to. I want to know what you find.'

Lewinder looked as surprised as Nelly had done.

4

It was morning, Stella was still asleep, but the Chief Commander was up and walking around. The cat and dog were wakeful with him, both watching him in hope of a meal or a walk. Or, in the case of the dog, of both.

He ignored them as long as he could, pacing the sitting room while he thought things through. He was furious that he had been attacked: angry with himself and with his attacker.

But it meant something: it meant that by visiting the house in Tolliver Street and the lodging house in Shambles Passage, off Brunswick Street, he had alarmed the killer of Joe and Josie. Which meant in turn that the houses were important.

Merry Trent had apparently lodged in Shambles Passage but had not been seen for some days. Popped in and popped out, Coffin thought. And what do we make of that? Ask brother Harry? I think not.

He went to make some coffee, to find himself followed into the kitchen by the two animals. The cat leapt up to a shelf, staring at him with a steady eye, while the dog leaned on his foot, lovingly and heavily.

'Oh, all right, you two. Food.' He opened the refrigerator door, stared at what he saw, and then removed a dish of cold chicken. He knew his Stella well enough to know she would not grudge the pair what was left. 'She probably meant it for you two,' he said. With quick slashing knife cuts, he carved the chicken into substantial pieces, put them on clean dishes and handed them out. Tiddles sniffed the offering carefully but on Coffin's firm advice started to eat before the dog finished his own dish and started on the cat's. Bob was not one to leave food waiting.

Coffin took a cup of coffee and went to stare out of the window at a dark grey sky in which black clouds raced. The cat leapt up, stretching out his head and neck for a caress. Coffin obliged. He was fond of Tiddles who had stayed by him through many a crisis. 'What are they going to find in that house, puss?' He let his hand wander over the soft fur. 'I think I know.'

Tiddles stared in his face as if he knew as well, but they were both interrupted by the sound of Stella's voice. Like all actresses of her generation she knew how to make a soft sound carry.

'Coming,' called her husband. 'I'll bring you some coffee.'

Stella was leaning against the pillows, contriving to look at once languid and lovely. Her hair was ruffled, she had no make-up on, she was no longer young, but no one and nothing could put down her beauty.

'Didn't know you were awake, here's some coffee. Made it myself.' He was proud of this skill and watched Stella's face anxiously while she took the first sip. Stella, denied what she considered good coffee, could be irritable.

'I've trained you to make really good coffee,' she said appraisingly.

'It's a great skill,' said Coffin, grateful for the accolade. He sat down on the bed, and the dog came too. He was not going to argue about who had taught him, although he thought he had taught himself.

'So what's going on?'

'Just work.'

Stella drank her coffee. 'It's Joe and Josie, isn't it? You can talk to me, it was in my theatre.'

Stella thought of St Luke's as 'her' theatre, in spite of the money that Coffin's sister had put in. But Letty was in New York, from which city she might come winging in at any minute.

'I wish I had got to know them,' said Stella over her coffee. 'They must have been an interesting pair. But why kill them? And in the theatre like that?'

'I expect there was a good reason.'

'Do you mean the murderer was someone who worked in the theatre?'

'It had to be someone who could move around freely.'

'Not an actor,' said Stella quickly.

'I didn't say that, it could have been a member of the audience.'

'Well, we don't watch them, that's true. People do get up and walk about sometimes. Is it known when they were killed?'

'They had not been dead long. I think it's reasonable to assume that they did not sit there dead or dying for very long. Of course, they didn't look dead. Say they were killed at or just about the end of the performance?'

'Did anyone see anything?'

'As far as I know, not. That would be too easy, wouldn't it? I haven't asked Lewinder, but his team will have been questioning the audience, they did a quick survey last night, and I think will go round checking up today.'

Stella yawned. 'I had a migraine last night, I went to bed early, didn't hear you come in.'

'I was late.'

He had gone to the hospital to have his wound dressed and then talked with Lewinder into the night.

Then Stella saw his bandaged wrist. 'What's that?' she asked sharply.

'Nothing too bad. I walked into a patch of trouble.'

'Is it part of this business?'

'Yes, you could say that.'

'I wish you'd keep out of things.' She leaned back against the pillows. 'I wish Archie Young was here. He'd tell me what was going on, you never do.'

'He'll be back. And I do tell you.'

'Only when you have to.'

There was enough truth in this to silence him.

'The truth is that you may be head of the Force, but at heart you are a working detective. You can't give it up, it's the way you live and breathe.'

'I want to clear this murder up and I begin to see the way forward.'

He took her cup from her and put his arms round her. 'Come on, Stella, say you understand.'

'I understand you all right, and I always have done.'

'I don't like the feel of this affair, Stella. I must get to the bottom of it.'

'You always take these things so personally.'

'It *is* personal with Harry Trent in it.'

Stella sat up. 'Are you sure he is? Aren't you jumping to a conclusion? You do sometimes, you know.'

'Thanks.'

'You don't like Harry, do you?'

Coffin took his time answering. 'Once I liked Harry very much, a good chap. But now he worries me. I don't trust him.'

'Why not?'

Coffin stood up and moved around the room. Stella had thrown her clothes around, a silk slip here, a pair of tights here, and on the table she had poured a pearl necklace with matching earrings. Yesterday's scent arose from them. Today she would probably use another scent, rosier and fresher than yesterday's, which was heavy with musk.

He looked at her. 'What was the scent you were wearing yesterday?'

She frowned. 'Jolie Madame, I think. Yes, that was it. I found an old bottle, it may have been stale. Does it worry you?'

'No, just curious.'

'Why don't you talk to Harry?'

'I will if I can find him.'

'He's moved in with Alfreda and Barnabas.'

'Did you fix that up for him?'

'No, although Alfreda came to tell me about it. They met in Max's and fixed it up. She had a room to let, he wanted somewhere to stay.'

'Quick,' commented Coffin.

Stella shrugged. 'I think they took to each other, and why not?'

Coffin bent over her. 'Goodbye, I'm off. It's going to be a tough day.'

'You look tired now.'

He looked exhausted, she thought. She watched his back as he closed the door carefully behind him. Tiddles slipped into the room as he left and leapt on to the bed.

'What is he not telling me, puss?' she said, reaching out to stroke the thick, rich fur. Since living with her and Coffin, Tiddles had grown a lustrous coat, changed from the ragged fur of his homeless days.

Alfreda Boxer said: 'Do you ever get the feeling that someone is talking about you?'

'Frequently,' said Harry Trent. 'And they usually are.'

They were sitting over breakfast in Alfreda's small kitchen. Barnabas was with them but he was reading a book and eating toast.

She rented a little flat near to the theatre. As she said herself, in a job where there was no security of tenure, she might be working in Edinburgh or Birmingham this time next year, so it was better to rent than to own. The kitchen was warm and comfortable with white-painted furniture and red check curtains. Alfreda had cooked them a breakfast of bacon and eggs.

'You got enemies?'

Harry thought about it. 'One or two. You pick them up in my way of work.' Then he said: 'What about you?'

'I don't know if I'm important enough to have enemies.'

'Oh, you don't have to be important,' said Harry with conviction. 'Believe me.'

Alfreda appraised the moment. 'It's the first time I've been close to a policeman.'

There was a pause. 'Are you close?' asked Harry.

'I could be,' said Alfreda.

'How long have you been thinking that?'

'Oh, I made up my mind quickly, you can bet on that.'

'I felt that.' He added, 'Might not be wise.'

'Oh, wise, who talks about wise?'

Harry did not answer. Perhaps theatre people were like

this, he told himself. And if so, how did John Coffin manage life with Stella Pinero. He had to admit he had always envied him his Stella. He loved his Lou, but things were not going well there at the moment, it might do them both good if he . . . He did not spell out exactly what would do them both good.

'I saw you around,' said Alfreda.

'Me or my twin . . . you may have seen him. Perhaps thought he was me.'

'Perhaps . . . I don't know about that,' said Alfreda.

'He isn't as nice as I am.'

'Oh, is that a warning?'

'You could say so.' Harry looked down at his plate.

Jekyll scented danger at that moment, although he did not like to admit it. I must not put my head out, he said to himself. But there was pressure, he was being pressed. There was a medieval punishment which involved heavy weights being placed on the victim's body. *Peine fort et dure.* This was it.

Harry stirred restlessly, disturbing Barnabas who got up and walked out of the room. 'Going to get a newspaper, see what they have to say about the murders.'

Harry looked up and said: 'Barney didn't like you saying that.'

Alfreda laughed. 'No, he's interested in the murders. I am too.' She went to the door and called after him: 'Bring me the papers too . . .' She came back and poured herself some more coffee. 'He reads a lot of detective stories and real-life crimes. It's one of his interests . . . Anyway, he knows I was only joking.'

'Was it only a joke?'

'What do you think?' Alfreda was smiling.

Harry said deliberately: 'I think I like a joke. And I could do with a good joke in my life, haven't found one lately. Not very funny the other night, was it? Did you know the pair that were killed?' He tried to read her face, but she turned away.

77

'Bought the odd hamburger and hot dog, we all have. What about you? I got the idea you did know them.'

'I thought I did, but as it turned out, they were strangers to me.' Harry heard himself say the words, and he repeated them under his breath: 'Strangers to me.' Aloud he said: 'People turn into strangers with time often, don't you think –?' He stopped himself. 'Joke.'

Alfreda drew back a little as if, jokes apart, she sensed danger. 'About your brother,' she began, then she stopped as Barnabas came back into the room.

He was excited, full of news.

'I met the postman . . . he says there are police cars parked outside the house in Tolliver Street where the Macintoshes lived and a guard on the front. The press are there too. Something's up. I'm going round.'

Alfreda took her cup and saucer to the sink where she dumped it. Harry had already decided that she was no housekeeper. 'Don't bother with the dishes,' she said. 'I will do them later. I must get to the theatre now to see what is happening. If anything. Will the police let us open?' Harry did not answer. Who was he to read the Chief Commander's mind? Or that of Superintendent Phil Lewinder, not a man of much imagination, he had thought. What a good thing the curtain had actually come down on that night.

Alfreda went through into the hall while Harry stood at the sink, washing the cups and saucers by holding them under the tap and letting the hot water run over them. They could dry by themselves. He had the idea that this was the usual method in Alfreda's casual household.

He heard her on the telephone. 'Right, Miss Pinero, see you in the theatre.' Her voice dropped, he had to strain to listen, which he did without shame. 'No, no trouble, he can stay as long as he likes. No, I'm fine and so is Barney.' That call ended and she began to talk to another person. 'Hello, May . . .' But he couldn't hear any more.

He went back to the sink and the dishes as he heard the receiver go down.

Alfreda came back into the room. 'You shouldn't be doing

that. A woman comes in, Mrs Freeman, and cleans up. I was only joking about leaving it all.'

Quite a joker, you are, Harry thought. 'I'll finish what I've started.' He looked up from the dishes. 'Rule of life.'

'Good rule,' said Alfreda, 'if you can carry it out.' She was carrying a briefcase and several books under her arm. A working day. 'I'll be eating a sandwich in the Workshop Bar, Max does a good one, at around midday, if you're looking for company.' She hesitated at the door; 'Stella's very discreet as a policeman's wife, but the murder in the theatre comes close to her. We are going to open . . . She says that a police team is tearing apart that house they lived in. Wonder what they are looking for?' She looked directly at Harry.

'Don't ask me.'

'Those Macintoshes, the dead couple. A puzzle, weren't they, when you think about it. They weren't what they seemed.'

'Who is?' And don't I know it, he thought.

'Just thought you would be interested. You could go and ask.'

'In case you haven't noticed, John Coffin has pushed me to the edge of the picture.'

But he took in what she had said, he finished washing the dishes, tidied the kitchen and himself, then walked all the way to Tolliver Street.

The street was partly blocked off with several cars, together with a van. He could not get close to the house but he saw Barney sitting on a low stone wall and joined him.

'What's going on?'

Barney, he seemed to be Barney at the moment, more agreeable than at breakfast, shrugged. 'Saw digging equipment going round the back. Digging the garden, I reckon.'

'You could be right.'

'Why don't you go and ask?'

'Wouldn't tell me. I've explained that to your mother.'

'Asking, was she?'

'So are you.'

'I'm interested in crime. It's a side of life . . .' He asked: 'What was Mum doing?'

'On the phone.'

Barney waited.

'Stella,' amplified Harry, 'then someone called May.'

'Oh, that will be May Renier. Everyone talks to her, she's wardrobe mistress, that puts her at the heart of things.'

Harry got up. 'I don't think there's any point in staying here.'

Barney said: 'I must get to the theatre soon, work calls.' But he kept his eyes on the house. He nodded his head to a car parked down Tolliver Street. 'See that red car . . . the press, I think. They think the police are on to something.'

Harry walked through the streets until he got to Max's café. It was open and already had a scattering of theatre people in it. He ordered some coffee, then went through to the telephone booth at the back.

He had the Chief Commander's office number, the number of the telephone that rang straight to his desk. If you were lucky, Coffin answered. He did now.

'Hello, this is Harry Trent. Listen, I just wanted to say that I think I know what you are looking for in Tolliver Street.'

Then he put the telephone down quickly and went to drink his coffee.

'He'll take that for a confession, I know he will,' he thought with bitter mirth, as he drank his coffee.

The police search of Tolliver Street went on all that day and into the next.

Towards evening, a telephone call went out to John Coffin.

'Think we have it, sir,' said Phil Lewinder. 'If you come round now, we can leave the final uncovering.'

'I'm on the way,' said John Coffin.

5

John Coffin was met in the hall of the old house by Phil Lewinder. There was a strange smell floating in the air.

'The dust of ages,' said Lewinder. 'We've turned up places that haven't seen the hand of man for years, decades, I should think.' He led the way down the hall. 'The dead couple just lived in three rooms as far as I can make out. Ignored the rest.'

'Did they own the house?'

'There's no rent book, but I doubt if they owned it.'

'Squatters?'

'In a curious kind of way, yes. Had to be. But we are checking, just a question of time. The legal department at the Parsons Road office is checking.'

'They are good,' said Coffin thoughtfully. He walked into the sitting room which was changed since his other visit: the floor was up with a big gaping hole in the middle.

'We found some bones underneath there . . . thought at first it might be a baby, but it turned out to be a cat . . . crawled in and got imprisoned, I think. Don't think it was deliberate. Hope not. Anyway, the guess is that it's a good fifty years old.' He was a cat lover. 'Still, that's not what I got you down here to see.'

'No, I know that.'

'I don't know how you got on to it, sir,' said Lewinder respectfully.

'Guesswork.' And nor am I the only one – Coffin was thinking about the call from Harry Trent. Harry, however, was probably not guessing but knowing.

'Isn't it always?' said Phil Lewinder, anxious to be obliging.

He didn't entirely believe what he said because although guessing certainly came into it, so did hard legwork. Interviewing witnesses, compiling reports, reading other people's reports, checking your own and their reports.

Also, listening to your boss, the Chief Commander, who was taking a strong interest in this double murder, and you asked yourself: Why?

Was it because the killing had taken place in his wife's theatre?

Or did it have something to do with Harry Trent? Now *that* was a name that interested him, and a man whom he was going to have to question.

He started, delicately, on the preliminaries: he wanted to feel his way forward with the Chief Commander.

'I learn that this house, strange as it seems now, was once used for children in need of care . . . not exactly a hostel, a big family home.'

He looked in Coffin's face to see what he read there.

'So I understand,' said Coffin, in a neutral voice.

'The records say it was run by a couple called Macintosh. Well, we've got two dead people who called themselves Macintosh . . . but they don't seem to match up with those earlier people.'

'Not at all, I'd say.'

'It's an interesting puzzle.'

Coffin moved forward. 'We've made a start in undoing it.' He pushed open the kitchen door. 'I see you've had the kitchen floor up . . . Find anything here?'

'No bones. A bundle of old clothes; forensics are looking them over just in case. You never know what's going to speak to you.' This sentence was aimed at Coffin who did not react. 'And a kid's possessions . . . Looks as though they were just thrown away here.'

'What sort? Toys?'

The superintendent pointed. 'Over there, sir, waiting to be photographed and inspected by the scientists . . . just in case.'

A football, a pair of boots, small in size, not for a big boy, a cricket bat and a pair of boxing gloves, small again.

'Don't know if they were hidden or just chucked down,'

said Lewinder. 'Either way,' he went on, his voice suddenly hard, 'it's an unpleasant picture . . . I don't think this was what you could call a happy house, sir.'

'But everyone seemed to like the Macs,' said Coffin. 'I did myself, the little I saw of them. But we didn't really know them, did we? I wonder what their real names were. We shall have to find out.' Thoughtfully, he said: 'I think the kid's possessions must predate the Macs, so called. Did they leave any papers, documents, letters?'

'Not found anything helpful as yet. A nameless pair, if you can believe it.'

'But someone must know.'

'Oh yes, we'll get there. Might take time, though.'

'Take all the time you want,' said Coffin absently. 'What about the bedroom?'

'That was the room that had most of the pair's possessions, they lived a pretty communal life, I'd say, shared everything. But that wasn't where we —'

'No, I'd have been surprised.'

'You don't seem surprised, sir. If you don't mind me saying so?'

'I'm never surprised,' said Coffin. 'Anything interesting in the bedroom?'

'Nothing special, sir, but we haven't finished going over everything . . . I wondered if Inspector Trent had anything cogent to say.'

Coffin liked the word cogent but decided not to say so.

Lewinder went on: 'I believe it was he who first pointed out that these were not the Macs he had known.'

'That's right. But no, he didn't point us in this direction, although he seems to have heard about the dig.'

'Everyone has. We shall have a crowd outside soon. Can't keep a search like this secret.' Lewinder looked at Coffin, wondering how to put what he had to say: after all, the Chief Commander seemed to know Trent from way back. 'Trent has a twin brother, I believe.'

'So he says.'

'Identical, too.'

'From the snatch of him in the video, they look very alike,

granted the different clothes. You've seen that picture, I assume?'

'Yes, sir. Could almost be the same person. Of course, it's that way with identical twins, I have identical twin cousins, can hardly tell them apart, but they are growing less alike.'

Coffin gave no ground. 'Let's get on with this. So there was nothing in the bedroom?'

'Can't say for sure as yet, there might be helpful material . . . something that will give a positive, real identification for Joe and Josie. They must be known somewhere. And we need to find out how they come to be living here.'

'So, where did you make your find? Show me.'

Without a word, Phil Lewinder led the way through the house and out into the garden.

The garden was as neglected as a garden could be, with a shaggy overgrown patch of grass – a lawn it could not be called – surrounded by a thicket of bushes and shrubs all growing into each other.

A narrow path ran down the middle of the grass. At the end of the path a canvas screen had been set up. A constable in his shirt sleeves stood close by.

'You been out in the garden before, sir?'

'Took a look when I came.'

'But you didn't walk down the path?'

Coffin shook his head. 'No.'

'If you had done, then I think you would have noticed the irregularity of the grass. Bumpy. As if the soil had been disturbed and dumped back in a casual way. Some time ago, so the grass had grown back, but you can see it.'

'I think I would have noticed it, yes' – he turned to the superintendent with a smile – 'and I like to think I would have seen the significance of it.'

'Well, it was easy for me, sir, you sent me looking.'

That's true, Coffin thought, I sent you looking and why did I do that? I did it because I walked around a sordid lodging house looking for a man who had been there, who had rented a room, was still renting it, but was not to be seen. Are you alive or dead? I asked. Or a ghost?

I could smell death.

'I thought it was worth a look round here, in this house, to see what you could find. If anything.'

There was a noise inside the house, both men turned round to see the cause of the disturbance.

'Oh, come through, Harry,' called out Coffin. 'It's all right, Constable, let Inspector Trent into the garden.' The uniformed constable dropped his hand from Harry Trent's arm.

'Sorry, sir, didn't know who you were.'

'No reason you should.' Harry gave himself a shake and walked into the garden. He addressed himself to Coffin. 'Thought I'd find you here, sir.'

'I wondered if you would come.' Coffin nodded towards the canvas screen. 'Want to see what we've got?'

Superintendent Lewinder was not pleased at the invasion, but he was not in a position to make difficulties if the Chief Commander accepted the visitor.

Trent stood where he was. 'Take a turn round the garden?' he said.

'Yes, sure.' Coffin accepted the need to talk. There was a strange look on Harry Trent's face. 'What is it?'

Harry walked a few paces forward before beginning, and even then he spoke with his back to Coffin. 'It's my brother, my twin, Merry . . . You're looking for him, aren't you?'

'I'd certainly like to find him, I think he needs to be found. What is this, Harry — you were looking for him yourself.'

Trent seemed on the edge of tears, as if the years had rolled away and he was a child again. He had found Merry a day or two ago, hadn't he? But a man could die and be buried fast in this part of London. 'Is he here?'

'If so, he has been dead long enough for the grass to grow over him.'

Trent went white. 'I love him.' There were tears in his eyes. 'And when I heard you were digging here . . .'

'If your brother died and was buried here in this garden, then he died as a boy, and I would have to ask you if you killed him, Harry.' Coffin gave Trent a push. 'Come on, let's go and have a look.'

They joined Lewinder, who had moved behind the canvas

screen. The earth had been dug down about three feet, a shallow enough grave.

'Nothing has been disturbed as yet,' said Lewinder. 'I'm waiting for the photographer before anything is touched.'

Coffin looked down. There below, with a scattering of earth still on the lower limbs, was a figure, clothed, the clothes as yet not completely rotted although the process was underway. The hands were crossed on the chest, large hands they had been, but skeletal now, with a watch still on the wrist and a large gold ring on the left hand, little finger.

The face had fallen away into a skull.

'Is that your brother?' asked Coffin.

Harry Trent was silent for a moment.

Superintendent Lewinder, who did not know what to make of this, said: 'Hard to make an identification just from a look.'

'It's a man, a fully grown male, judging by the size of the limbs.'

'It's not my brother,' said Harry Trent, 'but I know who it is. I recognize the ring, it used to leave a bruise when he beat us. It's Mr Macintosh.'

Without meaning to, he had fallen into the way of address he had used as a youngster.

Lewinder said: 'I think there is another body underneath.'

Coffin looked at Harry Trent. 'There would be, wouldn't there?' To himself, he added: They die in pairs round here.

He saw Harry Trent put his hand to his face. 'It has to be her.'

'Of course it does. But let's make sure.' Coffin nodded his head at the superintendent. 'Get on with it.'

He drew Harry Trent back. 'It will take some time; the first body has to be photographed and then moved. No doubt it is Macintosh the First, but we can't take anything for granted.'

'It's him all right,' said Harry in a toneless voice. 'And her underneath.'

'No doubt.' Coffin thought the same himself. 'Let's sit in my car. I want to talk to you.'

When they were settled, Coffin in the driving seat, with

Harry Trent leaning back against the seat next to him, his eyes closed, Coffin said: 'This has upset you.'

Trent did not answer. Coffin leaned forward to get out the small flask of whisky he kept in the dashboard drawer for occasions such as this. Once, he would not have trusted himself with a flask of whisky so easily to hand, but now he knew he was safe. Stella had given him the silver flask, chosen it at Asprey's in Bond Street, and had his initials chased on it.

He filled the top of the flask. 'Here, drink this.'

Harry Trent opened his eyes and took the drink. 'Nice object,' he mumbled as he looked at the flask.

'I always feel like an Edwardian gent out shooting when I use it.'

Trent drained the small, silver tumbler. 'They knew how to live then, all right.'

'You had to be rich to do it in style,' observed Coffin drily. 'This was a present to me.'

'From a woman,' said Trent; the whisky had gone to his head.

'Stella.'

'Sorry . . . I only meant it was a woman's present.'

'It's the sort of present theatre people give. I expect Stella's given things like it away by the dozen.' Probably not true, although he wouldn't count on it. But not with the same inscription on it.

Trent drew down the window on his side. 'What did you want to talk about?'

Coffin tucked the silver flask away; he was always careful with it. Anything that Stella gave him with such love was a sacred object.

'I was just having a thought.'

Trent turned round sharply. 'Surprise me.'

Coffin said thoughtfully, 'You might not like it, but let me share it with you.'

'I don't think I care for the sound of that.'

'Two boys, there were two, so you tell me, twins. I don't know how physically weak or strong you both were, let's settle for average. I think you would be strong enough to overpower and kill two people if you planned it right.'

'No. No, and no.'

'And then bury them. It's a shallow grave.'

'No. Don't go on.'

'Or perhaps it was just your brother's doing?'

Trent was silent. 'I think Merry could kill and he hated them, but I don't accept that he did.'

'Just considering the possibilities.'

He could feel Harry hating him at that moment, hate came out in warm waves, like an effluvium from somewhere base.

'I did not kill them, or help to kill them, or bury them. Does that cover it?'

Coffin considered. 'It does.'

'That's what I think.'

Coffin looked at him. Did Trent realize what a strange remark that was to end on?

He opened the car door. 'You get off. You're staying with Alfreda . . . Yes, I know. These things get around. So I know where to find you. Still looking for Merry?'

Harry Trent nodded without a word.

'Let me know if you find him.'

'Will do.'

Coffin watched as Trent walked away. 'There is a man who doesn't seem to know if he is one man or two.'

6

Stella, when she heard the news of the twin burials, was anxious. What would it mean for St Luke's Theatre, now renamed the Stella Pinero Theatre and its Theatre School? And especially to this present season, which was so important financially to the theatre and its plans. Would it keep people away, or bring them in? Temporarily, no doubt, there would be crowds. But would they be staring around them or buying tickets? 'Bums on seats, that's what pays wages,' she muttered to herself.

'What's that?' asked Coffin.

'Just voicing a worry.'

'Worried myself.'

They were together in Stella's former flat, vacated by Harry who had left no trace. Stella kept her clothes in her old bedroom in a long wall cupboard. 'I can move my body into your place easily enough,' she had said to Coffin, 'not my clothes.' Stella took her clothes seriously: chiffons and soft silks hung together at one end, the fabrics moving up in stiffness and heaviness through rich silks to soft woollens to tweeds. Not many tweeds: Stella, after many experiments, had decided she was not really a tweedy person. 'It's a question of hips,' she had explained once. 'My hips aren't really tweedy. I'm not lean and long enough.' She was not regretful: she had done well as she was.

'Two dead bodies in the theatre and two bodies buried not far away. All with the same name.'

'As far as we know,' said her husband. He was slumped in a chair, watching his wife sort out her clothes. He was there by invitation, he never took liberties with his Stella, he had learnt that lesson the hard way. But today she had wanted him there.

For his sake as well as her own: she was concerned. All right, he had professional worries, everyone had those, he lived with problems. He lived with blackness, bloody tragedies and despairs, but that was his working life and the good policeman knew how to separate himself, become detached. Not all the time, perhaps, but most of it.

He could usually talk to her. In fact, as he had once said, she was the only person he could talk to with freedom, he had no one else.

But she felt now, he had a deep anxiety inside him that he was not expressing to her.

She looked at him with care: perhaps he had gone off her, and was secretly fancying someone else. It was something you always had to take into account. Not that Phoebe woman, she hoped. But there was no evidence of it, and she flattered herself that she would not be easy to deceive.

She pulled a short flutter of black chiffon from its hanger to gaze at it with respect.

'Nice dress,' he said.

Stella patted it. 'That's a Chanel. Very nearly a Chanel, almost a Chanel.'

'Looked in the door of the atelier, did it? Breathed the air and walked away?'

Stella ignored this sally. 'I lent it to Deborah Masters so she could audition for Johnny Whiteman when he was producing his new show.'

'And what happened?'

'She died,' said Stella with regret as she rehung her precious relic.

'What?' Coffin sat up.

'Oh, not your sort of dying, although she did that later, too, poor love. No, she died on stage, lost the words, failed the audition.'

'Ah.' He sat back. 'Nothing I have to worry about.'

'No, natural causes the coroner said.'

'Oh, there was a coroner?'

'Mmm, well, she was dead in the corner at a party. Now

that wasn't like Deb. Usually the life and soul. But she choked apparently on a bit of kebab. She was still holding the stick in her hand. She was a rabid anti-vegetarian too, poor love, and it was a piece of chicken that stuck. Bird power striking back. No one heard her choking, it was a very noisy party.'

He laughed, then said: 'Did you invent that?'

'Well, bits of it, not all: she is dead and she did choke, but it was on a piece of toffee and in the quietness of her own bedroom. Although come to think of it,' Stella added thoughtfully, 'that wasn't always so quiet.'

Coffin laughed again.

Come, Stella thought, that's not so bad. 'Would you like a drink? Coffee, tea, or something stronger?'

Without waiting for an answer, she went into the kitchen. Presently there was a pop, and then a scream from Stella. 'Help, it's frothing all over me.'

Coffin went out into the kitchen. Stella did little cooking, it was not expected of her, she said, and what small amount she performed took place in the tower where she now lived with Coffin, but she had always kept something to drink, and she was enough a child of her time to enjoy champagne. But it had to be good, vintage stuff.

There she was now, holding the bottle which had spurted all over. 'It's having an orgasm,' she said. 'Here, you pour.'

Coffin took the bottle with a mild, reproving look – he had a slight puritanical streak which manifested itself in relation to his wife. Stella had none and she giggled. 'Why champagne?' There was nothing to celebrate, rather the reverse.

'I thought you needed cheering up and I certainly do: a quartet of corpses is no benefaction.'

Coffin nodded, as he poured the champagne for them both. 'I won't say cheers,' he said gloomily.

'You think Harry Trent is in it, don't you?'

Coffin was quiet for a moment. 'Wish I knew. And about brother Merry. I'd like to lay eyes on him.' Did he exist?

Stella unloaded one of her worries. 'Are we going to be able to run the show? . . . I understood about being closed for a time, and anyway it would not have been decent to have played. But, as they say, the show must go on.'

'Yes. I knew you would want to.'

'We need the money. So when?'

'I've cleared it with Lewinder and he says you can go ahead. Of course, the area round the box will be covered in.'

'Thank goodness.' Stella gave a shudder. She genuinely felt distaste, but perhaps the gesture had a theatrical flourish, it was second nature to her now to perform. Or, perhaps, as someone had once said, it was her first and only nature, that she was a theatrical animal through and through and had probably acted in the cradle. Coffin himself half agreed with this judgement; he did not mind, in fact, he loved her for it.

She gave the conversation a slight shift. 'Do they know how the two in the theatre were killed?'

'Stabbed.' Coffin was cautious. 'Still being studied.'

'Oh.' Stella considered. 'Does that mean the killer had special knowledge? A doctor, or a nurse?' After a moment's thought, she added: 'Or a soldier?'

'Not necessarily. You'd be surprised how easy it is to pick up knowledge of that sort. A bit of luck might be needed for the actual performance, I admit that.'

'Have you found the weapon?'

'No, not yet. May never do.'

'What was it like?'

'Thin, narrow, at least at the penetration point . . . that's how it seems. Exactly what we don't yet know. A very sharp knife. Longish, though.'

'There are bayonets in the current production,' said Stella.

'We thought of that, they are plastic.'

'I understand that we had a soldier round, checking on drilling,' said Stella carefully. 'I didn't see him myself, but he was around some days. Well liked, I believe.' She took a long drink of champagne and looked at him over the glass.

'Yes, Sergeant Peter Driver. He hasn't been overlooked. Lewinder is a careful chap, Driver will be questioned.'

'I have heard,' said Stella even more carefully than before, 'that he was talking about how you could kill. Over a drink, you know, quite casually.'

'Thanks,' said Coffin. 'You realize that might put the killer among your crew?'

Stella bent her head in acknowledgement. 'Thought of it myself. Couldn't miss it, really. A lot of extras for *Oh What a Lovely War*, not all professional actors.'

'Right. I'll bear that in mind.'

'If you would.'

Stella ran her hand across her dresses, feeling the ones she liked most. 'I love you,' she said.

With affectionate amusement, Coffin said: 'That wasn't our subject.'

'It always is, really, isn't it?'

He felt like saying : Heaven forbid, but he knew what she meant, it was just her way of saying it, that touch of the theatre that he half loved and yet half feared. Like J. B. Priestley, he was never sure that the link between religion and the theatre had been broken and he feared the link with magic, otherness, call it what you will, that he hadn't got himself. It did not always operate with Stella but it could be there.

What she meant now was: You don't have to tell me all that is in your mind, because I very often know. I know now that you are in trouble of which you do not speak.

He got up, stroked her hair, and kissed her cheek. 'I'm off. Be in touch.'

You certainly will, said Stella to herself. I will see to that, you need me around. I can read your mind, not letter for letter but the general burden.

True, it works both ways. Symbiosis.

Of course, you could call it successful sex, she added as she walked into the theatre, but we won't.

Stella went first to her office where her secretary was waiting for her with her post, of which there was always plenty.

She riffled through the pile. 'How much rubbish today, Philly?'

Philly Gray shrugged, she was part time but worked as hard as if she had been paid for forty-eight hours a day. 'Average. One lunatic wants to kiss the ground you walk on. I'd keep out of his way if I were you, but it shouldn't be difficult because the postmark was Osaka. Another writer would like to take tickets for all the current productions but he, it is a he, would like to take you out to dinner before or after each one. I'd give that a miss too, it would take up a terrible amount of your time.'

All this was delivered with a straight face so that Stella never knew when Philly was joking or not. It was one of the difficulties of dealing with her. The other was that she was too good for the job and both parties knew it. There has to be a balance in any relationship for it to work well, and Stella felt this was not so between her and Philly. To put it bluntly, Philly liked her a great deal more than she liked Philly. Philly was in love with her but no one said this aloud.

After Stella had dealt with her letters and made one or two telephone calls, she went along to the rehearsal room where she wanted to map out the decor for the next play she was involved in: she had just started directing; she had always dabbled, but now it was serious. All actresses need a second career as they get older and Stella meant to make this hers.

Here she found Barnabas, staring gloomily at the painting on the floor he was about to clear up. He had already discovered that being an assistant stage manager meant that he did all the tasks no one else wanted, as well as making cups of tea and doing the shopping for the performers.

Knowing his ways, and having suffered in the past, she waited for him to declare who he was today.

'Barney here,' he said without looking up from the floor. 'I think I always will be, I believe I know who I am now.'

Oh good, Stella thought. She liked stability.

'What's this?' She was looking at several strange shapes in bright colours on the floor. They didn't look human, nor like anything else much either.

'Lukey thought he'd paint backdrops of all the furniture he wanted for *Amber is For Ever*. Nothing real, you see, all painted and flat.' Luke Head was doing one production for them in between films. A short stay with Lee Strasberg in New York some years ago had made him determined to be innovative. He was putting his own money into it, which he could well afford, being a much-loved and highly paid film actor. Being also a good businessman, he intended to appear himself, knowing his face would draw the punters in. 'Make 'em rehearse with it.'

'And what's that strange shape you are wiping out?' It looked like a kangaroo with four legs.

'A dining table, it looked better before I started work on it, and that's a bookcase.' He pointed to a long narrow object.

'And those white and black shapes are meant to be the books?'

'That's right. And he had them picking them off the shelves as well. Clever mime.' He smiled at her. 'I like your husband.'

'So do I.'

'I wish I could work with him.'

'Be a policeman?'

'No, a detective. I'm interested in people, like to study them.' He stood up. 'Makes your bones ache doing this . . . they don't know how lucky they are, this lot, having this decent room to rehearse in and not some dud church hall.' He went on: 'That detective that's living with us. I think my mother fancies him. Otherwise she wouldn't have him in the house. That's what I think.' He frowned. 'Not the type she usually goes for.'

Stella kept quiet; she quite liked Harry Trent herself.

Barney relaxed his frown and gave judgement. 'I think he's crackers, mad, you know.'

'There is that possibility.'

'Is he gay?'

Stella did not answer immediately. 'Never thought about it,' she said at last. 'Why do you want to know?' Silly question, she thought. Only two answers and you could supply both of them.

'Just wondered.'

'And you're not?'

Barney gave her a serious look. 'Dunno. Not sure about it, not sure about anything. I'll find out. Or someone will show me. In time. Time counts, doesn't it? Answers most questions.'

'Usually too late,' said Stella.

Barney got down on his knees again. 'Better get on with this, I've got a list of jobs as long as my arm this morning.'

'You're a hard-working boy – Max tells me you help out there as well.'

Barney kept his eyes on the task in hand. 'Can't live on theatre money. I got ambitions.'

'You're a boy to keep an eye on,' said Stella absently, her thoughts really on her morning of hard work, as well as the duet of deaths. She knew these ambitious young actors: before you knew where you were, they were winning Oscars and handing you a supporting film part. That, or they were dead.

'Make haste with this, please, because I shall be needing this floor myself soon.'

As she turned away, he called: 'About Trent . . . don't suppose he is, but as they say, I think he would help out if they got busy.'

Stella shook her head at him, even as she laughed. He lowered his head and then she heard him say quietly, to himself, 'You're a lovely lady, Stella Pinero. A lady to love, I think I do.'

Stella heard, hesitated. Should she react or not? No, ignore it, you have not heard.

Then she left to go back to her office. On the way, she passed the dress store.

'Must have a look in there later, check up. We might be able to use the longer dresses for my production of *Private Lives*.' Economy was always necessary.

When in doubt, and with a hole in the programme, always do a vintage Coward was a theatrical truth that Stella clung to, especially if it is a play with only four characters (five, if you count the maid), one of which she intended to play herself.

She went to work, and Barney finished his cleaning-up operation then joined his mother in her cramped workroom.

'She said I was a boy worth watching.'

'If she knew you like I do, then she wouldn't take her eyes off you.'

Barney laughed. 'Shall I make us a cup of tea, Mum?'

'Yes, and make it strong.'

'The big brown pot?'

'Yes, and fill it up.'

'Good, right, Mum.'

He hummed as he filled the kettle, it was a good sign to use the big brown pot. They took the big pot round with them from job to job, it was their Ark of Covenant almost. He did not quite know what that meant, but it sounded good.

'Warm the pot,' called Alfreda after him.

'Warm the pot, warm the pot,' sang Barney in a low voice. 'I am the boy who always warms the pot.'

'What are you singing about?'

'Not singing, chanting.'

'You'll never make a fortune with your voice.'

Not trying, Barney said to himself, not trying.

'I hate your voice.'

'Not you, Mum, you love it. I am your baby boy.'

'You can cut that out.'

'Right, Mum. Out it goes. How many for tea?'

'Monty might look in. He's got some problem he wants to talk about.'

'Walking problem himself, that man.'

Stella worked away hard at her routine work, wondering, as she always did when so engaged, why she had allowed herself to create this theatre with its burdens that took her away from her true love of acting. But she knew the answer; ambition. All the same, it would have been good if Letty Bingham (only she had married again and was now Bingham Lacy, and there was a name before Bingham if only Stella could remember what it was), sister to John Coffin and whose money had provided most of the capital, would be more a part of it.

Letty had been pretty much an absentee lately and when Stella had complained to Coffin, he had pointed out that it seemed to be the habit of the women in his family. Look at his mother, going off when he was a boy, thought to be dead, but really going to an active and enterprising life in which she produced a Scottish brother for him, and Letty herself, the youngest and probably the cleverest and certainly the richest.

Stella raised her head from her work, realizing she had had no lunch and she was hungry and thirsty.

Silly to react because a lad said he loved her. He was good-looking though.

She worked on quietly for a while longer, then she remembered that she had wanted to check over what they called the 'surplus wardrobe', in other words, the set of cupboards where good but not-much-used gowns, suits, and robes were stowed away. She knew for a fact that there were several Falstaffs in there and one or two Hamlets. Ophelias tended to get used time and time again under other names in other plays.

She tidied her desk, collected her bag and briefcase and set off for a look.

The SP, as the surplus wardrobe was known, was located in a short passage which was only lighted when needed for economy's sake. You pulled a cord and the light came on.

She rolled back the long white door to SP and stepped inside, putting on the light as she did so. The clothes were arranged in a long row, packed tight.

She went down the line, pulling out this garment and that, assessing what she saw against what she needed, making mental notes before passing on.

Behind the front row was, as she well knew, yet another, hung with even older, dusty, mustier garments, inherited or bought in from defunct theatres. She always felt the ghosts of dead productions, forgotten shows, triumphs perhaps in their day, strongly in her nose as she came to these garments.

She sneezed as she pushed her way through. Not many people came here, so the air was heavier.

Beyond even these relics was one small rack of long-neglected outfits, but she recalled seeing a thirties-ish cocktail dress that might be revived. She had thought it pretty then, and now as she looked she still did so.

Tucked away behind it was a long black velvet robe with wide hanging sleeves. Handsome in its way, but probably of no use for *Private Lives*.

She picked it up and saw that the sleeves were lined with white satin. Had been white. Off-grey now with streaks of red.

She looked again. The red was blood.

And down the front of the gown was a spatter of little red spots.

Stella rolled up the velvet robe, and went back to her office, where she telephoned her husband.

'Can I come and see you?'

He was as welcoming as he ever was when at work. 'I'm busy.'

'Are you on your own?'

'Yes.' He sounded surprised. 'As much as I ever am here. What is it?'

'I want to show you something.'

'What?'

'Let me just show you.'

Because, she said to herself, as she hurried towards her car, this blood is not old blood.

Her husband was pleased to see her, although he tried to hide it.

He looked, she thought, thin, and as though at the back of his mind was something he did not want to think about.

'I like the new blue the room's done in,' she said, as if it was what she had come for.

'It's not so different from the old blue,' said Coffin. 'And there is still the old blue carpet and I don't much like blue. Come on, Stella, what is it?'

Without another word, Stella unrolled the black velvet gown before him.

'I found it in the SP wardrobe store. It was half hidden at the back. I was going to make use of it, then I saw . . .'

She pointed to the blood.

'Small spots up the skirt, and a streak inside the sleeve . . . that's where the weapon was hidden.'

Coffin took it from her to carry it to the window where he examined it carefully. Then he turned to her.

'You know you shouldn't have touched it. You should

have left it there and told one of the investigating team.'

'I couldn't find one, there was no one around. There never is when you want anyone . . . But I thought you would be pleased.'

Coffin looked at her, and smiled. 'I am, of course. Clever you.'

'They can still dig around in the back and look for all those forensic traces you go on about but which never seem to help all that much.'

Did she understand the implications of her find, he wondered.

'You realize that this places the killer right inside the theatre company? Someone who knew their way around?'

'It's not hard to work out that there are clothes behind that door if it's what you are looking for,' said Stella. 'There is a big notice on the door and another telling you to close the door and turn off the light. No genius is needed and you don't really need to be part of the people who work there.'

She was being defensive and he didn't blame her.

'Almost anyone could drop in and have a look round, our doorman works hard but he isn't always there. We need another really, but I can't afford it.'

Defensive again, he thought.

'Suggests at least a person who knows the theatre.'

Stella nodded. It was hard to say no to that.

'And someone who knew the Macintosh couple and knew they would be there. Perhaps sent them the tickets.'

Stella was silent.

'And had a motive for murdering them,' went on Coffin.

'There might be several people who fitted all those categories.'

'Sure.' He was silent for a while, looking at the velvet robe. 'This garment is big . . . Could fit a man or a woman. Change their appearance and allow them to slip the weapon up the sleeve.'

'That's what I thought.'

'Did you look for the weapon?'

Stella shook her head. 'It won't be there.'

'How do you know?'

'It just won't be.'

He came back and sat down to look at her. 'As it happens, I agree with you.' He put the gown on the desk in front of him. 'And shall I tell you why? It's because when we find the weapon, it will give us a lead straight away to the killer's identity. The weapon that killed those two people was a very individual and strange one. Thin, pointed and very sharp . . . When we get it, then it will give us a name. The murderer was not going to leave that weapon around for us to find.'

'How long were they dead?'

'To the point as ever, Stella' – he was not usually sharp with her which told her something, but she was not sure what – 'but the answer to what you mean is that they were almost certainly killed very soon after taking their seats.'

'Exactly how did they die?'

Coffin moved some papers on his desk. 'We haven't had the inquest yet . . . But each received a stab through the base of the skull. Not much blood, but some. They would have died quickly.'

'So they sat there, dead, all through the performance,' said Stella broodingly.

Coffin was silent.

'And probably the killer was around too,' she went on. 'Taking off the robe, hiding it . . . Perhaps hiding himself.'

'Or taking his seat in the audience,' said Coffin.

'Yes, or even going on stage.' She was quiet for a bit. 'No, I can't believe that. I don't believe you could perform after killing. I couldn't.'

'No, you couldn't.' He sat there looking at her with love and a streak of sadness. 'So a member of the audience or backroom staff or someone who got away. There is no evidence yet, as far as I know, one way or another.'

'What do you think?'

Coffin shrugged. 'If I have to guess: a member of the audience.'

'So we are back to it: a member of the audience, who knows something about the theatre, or has made a good guess, and who also knew the Macintoshes . . . because it is not just a random killing, is it?'

Coffin answered at a tangent: 'We might get a profile of the likely killer done.'

It was fashionable at the moment to commission such profiles, useful in some cases, not in others. It was not a fashion to which Coffin subscribed.

Stella recognized a non-answer when she heard one. She stood up.

'I'll let you get back to work. See you later.' At the door, she said: 'You think it might be Harry Trent.'

She did not make it a question, and she got no answer.

'I thought twins could kind of read each other's mind, knew what the other was doing.'

'Apparently this doesn't work with Harry and his brother Merry,' said Coffin drily.

'Might even mirror each other's actions,' Stella went on, as if he hadn't spoken.

'I believe with some twins it is so.'

Grumbling away to herself, Stella kissed his cheek and left.

Coffin watched her go, and knew he ought to have done more to help her. But the truth was that he needed help himself.

He had known Harry on and off for years, he had never known his twin Merry – if he existed, which to Coffin's way of thinking was not clear – but he had not thought of him as violent.

But he saw now that there were depths in Harry Trent that he had not been aware of, and that hidden in that deep Sargasso Sea of emotion might be hate.

And from hate, death could come so easily.

Stella drove back to the theatre in her usual competent way, even though her mind was not on the road, and she caused one taxi driver to shake his head at her.

As she parked the car, she remembered with dismay that she had left a portfolio with vital and confidential papers in it on the floor of the SP wardrobe. With a muttered curse at herself for being forgetful, she made her way there.

Out of the corner of her eye, as she went, she thought she saw a familiar figure. Someone she might recognize with a proper look. But she was in a hurry, so she rushed on, not wanting to meet anyone.

The short corridor was dark and empty, as usual. She pulled open the door, not bothering to put on the light because she knew that she had deposited her portfolio on the floor near to the first line of garments.

She had her hand on it, when she felt a presence.

It was nothing more than a sensation that someone was there, but it was strong. The feeling you get walking down a dark street when footsteps behind seem to follow you.

She drew back and began to turn away.

A slight movement of air ruffled her hair, made it untidy, and she put her left hand up to her head.

Hyde springing out from Jekyll, out again and in control, had done what had to be done in the circumstances. Hyde–Jekyll was the creature of circumstance, created by them, drawn out by them, made by them.

Hyde, with blood on his hands, did not mind spilling more. He found the smell enticing.

7

Jekyll—Hyde was a neat, well-dressed person. The underneath person was less neat inside but this did not show, except by a tremor that sometimes touched the hands, not so much a tremble as a quiver of the little finger on the right hand and the forefinger on the left. Did it mean something, should you read a symptom or a warning? Hard to say, but it possibly reflected a tremor in the brain (left brain, right brain at odds?) that would be translated into action of a horrid sort.

The person of Hyde, the physical apparatus was always well groomed. No disorder here. A certain Bohemian style occasionally, yes, but that was permitted. Hyde, after all, was not obliged to wear a uniform.

Jekyll and Hyde did not talk to each other, did not converse, but there must have been communion underneath. Had to have been. They had had one placenta between them, after all.

Hyde was silent as a rule, he never sang and rarely spoke, it was wiser so. He could speak but he chose to be reserved. Jekyll sometimes sang, not exactly through happiness but more through pain as if he could feel Hyde trying to force his way back in. The reverse of giving birth is bound to be painful.

Hyde thought he could escape from Jekyll: Jekyll knew that he never could, the cord that had held them in infancy, held them still.

And for ever, he thought. They would die as they had been born.

They had both of them, he thought, struggled for separate

life: drawn apart, come back together again, despaired at being like two persons standing on one foot.

Jekyll, the more respectable of the two, sometimes wondered if it would be easier if they were of a different sex. Possibly Hyde could change? Perhaps had already done so, sex was not at all as stable with some people as was imagined. There could be a kind of shifting, he thought, which might settle things down.

Idle thought, Hyde was not one for changing. He knew, deep down, of Jekyll's exceedingly hostile thoughts and wondered if Jekyll would turn murderer of Hyde.

It could be done.

But no, Hyde was the killer and Jekyll the good one. Goodish, anyway.

I am the dealer of death, Hyde thought, it is my mission, Jekyll just keeps the book.

A pleasing thought that: Jekyll, the good one, the law keeper, the keeper of the book of death.

8

Coffin was interrupted almost immediately after Stella left him by an unwelcome telephone call. Not one he wanted at all, but one that he knew had to come. He was only glad that she had not been in the room with him when the telephone on his personal, not-exactly-secret-but-private line rang.

She would have listened, and asked questions.

He listened with care but without pleasure.

'You want to run over a few things?' he questioned bleakly. Thought they'd done that. Tests and tests already. What the hell was this?

Questions, it seemed. He was usually the one who asked the questions and did not care for this reversal of roles. Now he knew how his subjects felt. When were the results of those earlier tests coming in? Soon. What sort of an answer was that?

His throat felt as scorched as his mouth. A drink of whisky would be the thing. And once it would have been his way out, but not any longer. He had tried it once and knew his vulnerability.

He put the receiver down, and let himself give a deep groan, short but satisfying, and felt better at once.

It was better not to bottle things up. If he felt strong enough he might even talk to Stella tomorrow. Take her out to lunch, she would like that.

On cue, as if she had been waiting for him to finish his call, which probably she had been, his secretary, the fat new one, bustled in. She did bustle, no harm meant, but it irritated him.

She deposited a pile of reports, letters and flimsy message slips on the desk in front of him, gave him a sympathetic smile and said that there was an urgent telephone call waiting and could she put it through?

Coffin nodded. And soon found himself involved in a long discussion on finance. And what was so urgent about that, he asked himself. Money could always wait around, couldn't it? But apparently it could not, it was more mobile than he had imagined.

Must be why he had never had any; it had been walking off while he was still thinking.

The phone call seemed to go on and on.

When he had finished, he looked at his watch. Nearly seven, not late by police hours, you did what you had to do. Or he did.

Then he remembered the robe that Stella had left with him.

'Damn.' He should have done something about that before this. Still, not important. Probably not important.

So he telephoned the superintendent's room; Lewinder was not there, but he got a young sergeant who sounded surprised to hear the Chief Commander's voice.

Surprised but not nervous. Cocky young devil, not how he would have been in his day. But then, come to think of it, he had never heard his Chief Officer's voice. Top brass kept themselves to themself in those days.

He explained the matter briefly to Sergeant Walker, asked him to send for the robe and suggested, tactfully, he hoped, that the wardrobe be examined again.

Just as well, really, that he was not talking to Lewinder.

Sergeant Walker considered matters, then walked across to the Chief Commander's office himself. He never missed an opportunity to make his mark where it mattered, and you never knew.

As it happened, he met no one: no one of importance, that is, only a couple of secretaries, the fat one whom he did not know, and the pretty fair one who was married.

Then he telephoned Superintendent Lewinder, who had

gone home because his wife was having friends to dinner.

'Where is the blood?'

'Sleeve, inner sleeve, sir.'

Lewinder swore, told him to get the robe photographed and then sent over to forensics, and then to get the clothes cupboard examined.

Carefully.

'There's not much blood on the robe, sir,' said Walker. 'It may not be anything to do with us. Someone cut themself or had a nose bleed.'

'Well, find out.' Lewinder's voice came over sounds of laughter and yes, the pop of a bottle.

Good party, thought Walker a little sourly. He accepted his mission, looked about for some support, but there was no one much around.

He sent off the necessary instructions to the photography unit. Then he deposited the gown in a locked drawer against the forensic examination (tomorrow it would be, that lot were inclined to take their time, complaining of overwork) and, with a feeling of virtue, he decided to go down to the canteen for a cup of tea and slice of toast first. He liked his food, and there could be no hurry. Not to speak of, surely.

The canteen was empty except for a pal with whom he sat for a few minutes, exchanging gossip.

Then he went over to the theatre, driving himself carefully through the thick traffic.

A performance was halfway through, but there seemed no one about in the front of the house, although he could hear the performers and there was the smell of activity on the air.

He had spent enough time in the theatre the last day or two to know his way around backstage. It had been he, as it happened, who had taken a quick look inside on the first day of the investigation.

More activity here backstage, of course, but no one took particular notice of him. He muttered to the young stage manager that he had to take a look at something and made his way through the corridors to where the cupboard had to be.

Yes, there it was.

As he advanced towards it, he considered what he knew: not much blood had been spilt in the killing, it had been a small, neat stab wound in each case.

So the blood on the sleeve, if it related to their deaths at all, which personally he was doubtful of, then it must have come from the killer.

Or the weapon. This latter idea the most likely.

There was the cupboard. He was about to open it when something on the ground caught his eye.

The carpet here was stained and worn, but the mark looked like blood.

He bent down. Yes, it was blood. He reached out a fore-finger to touch. His finger came away with a red stain on it.

The blood was wet. Just about, thick and clotting, but still moist.

The blood was wet where no blood should be.

But blood can come from anywhere, many sources: a nose bleed, a deep cut (because this blood was thickish, as if it had run freely), nor did it even need to be human.

Come to think of it, he told himself, this was a theatre, it could be stage blood.

No, it smelt wrong for that. Walker was a man who set a store by his own physical reaction, this smelt, he thought, like recently spilt human blood.

He had not been standing there many seconds as all these thoughts rushed through his mind, they were pushing at each other as they came, elbowing each other out of position.

He opened the door to the wardrobe; it stuck. He put his arm round the edge to give it a shove, he had to give it a push, because something was obstructing it. He got his right foot inside where it touched the obstruction, which felt soft.

He frowned. Didn't like that softness.

The wardrobe was better described as a small room with racks in it. The door opened inward.

Walker shoved more gently now at what was stopping him, he did not want to damage whatever was there. When he had enough of a gap he looked inside. The light from the corridor showed him that a figure was lying on the floor, half underneath one of the racks of clothes, hidden in the skirts of a long dress.

He pulled back the clothes to see who was there. A woman was lying on her face, her hair was bloody. He put his head close to her, she was breathing.

Gently, because head injuries were tricky, he turned her over. Her face was bloodstained, she had been bleeding from the nose.

A bad sign with a head injury.

He was kneeling by her, putting his thoughts together, when he heard the brisk patter of footsteps down the corridor.

A tall, slender woman, with a fall of gleaming hair, and a pair of large spectacles on a face that might have been lovely when truly young, but was still handsome. He knew who she was, if she recognized him she did not say so.

She gave a cry, letting go of the pile of papers she was carrying and dropping to the floor beside him. 'Good God, it's Madam!'

He stared at her, wordlessly.

'The boss. Miss Pinero.'

She touched Stella's cheek with a gentle finger. 'What's happened?'

'We had better get help,' Walker said, not answering.

Miss Pinero, Stella Coffin. Not a theatregoer, he had not recognized her. But who would, he thought, on the floor, in a cupboard, with all that blood. Alive, though.

'Who are you? Did you do this?' She drew back.

'No.' Bleakly, he explained himself and produced his identification which Alfreda accepted cautiously, keeping half an eye on him while she read it. 'You must have seen me around.'

Alfreda stood up. 'We must move her.'

'No, better not to move her. I don't know how badly hurt she is.' Or how.

'So what do we do?' She spoke as if she still didn't quite trust him.

Walker looked at her. 'I'm Alfreda Boxer,' she said in a

low voice, as if aware that she too needed explanation. 'I work here.'

Then she turned her head. Another person was coming down the corridor.

She called out. 'Barney . . .'

'Mum.'

A tall young man with a shock of hair was moving towards them. Walker could see a likeness to Alfreda.

'Mum, what's happened?'

I wish he wouldn't call me that, makes me feel a hundred, she thought. I don't like his expression. He's upset. Barney came up close.

'It's Stella,' he said. 'Miss Pinero . . . What's happened to her?' He sounded distressed. 'Is she dead?' He knelt down. 'Oh, she must be, mustn't she?'

Walker did not answer. He moved away from Stella's body, she was still breathing. 'Miss Boxer, stay here. I will do some telephoning.'

Alfreda unhooked a telephone from her belt. 'You can do it here.'

'With an injury like that,' said Barney, as if to himself. 'Oh, Stella, Stella.'

'She's not dead.' Alfreda was watching Walker who had moved away, out of earshot, and was talking on the phone. 'Not yet.'

'She's far away, though.' He knelt beside her, stroking her wrist. 'Stella, Stella, can you hear me? . . . I don't think you can.' He sat back on his heels. 'She'll slip away, I know she will, wordless.'

'She's still breathing.'

'Yes, you are, aren't you, Stella, darling?'

'I didn't know you were so fond of her.'

'Mum, what are you saying? She's dying.'

'Do you think so?' She still had her eyes on Walker, now returning.

'Yes.' Barney took Stella's hand in his. 'Her hand is chill.'

Walker said: 'Ambulance is on its way.'

'Stella, darling, hang on,' said Barney. 'She's far away, but they say that the hearing is the last to go . . . I'm here, Stella,

111

this is Barney . . . Who did this to you? Did you see?'

'Do be quiet,' said Alfreda.

'No, she may hear me . . . I don't suppose she does know, did know, who hit her . . .'

Walker leaned against the wall while he waited for the ambulance. Stay with her, he had been told, we will be with you in about ten minutes.

Alfreda and Barney, he told himself. She's his mother. Nice-looking woman, bet she smokes a lot, you can tell by her skin. What about him? Lanky boy, tall and thin, shock of hair, nice colour, though. Too much hair, but it's either too much or cut to the scalp at the moment. Wonder what they do here?

'I'm an administrator,' said Alfreda, as if she read his thoughts. 'Not an actress.'

Walker nodded. 'I was wondering.'

'I'm an assistant stage manager . . .' Barney smiled. 'Very low form of life. I do want to perform though, and I will in the end.'

It didn't seem right, Walker thought, for him to be passing personal information across when the boss's wife was lying there, possibly dying.

He could hear distant sounds as of clapping; a drift of music, a remote ripple of laughter: theatre sounds. Life going on.

He bent over Stella. Training had taught him to place her on her side so that she did not choke. She was still alive, he was sure of that, but he didn't like that blood that had come down her nose.

'I wonder who did this?' said Alfreda. 'And why? Why attack Stella?'

Walker did not answer. What was she doing here? And why was she so savagely attacked? Well, why am I here, he asked himself. I was looking for a possible murder weapon. She came to this wardrobe; God knows what brought her here, but she must have been here when the killer . . . it had to be the killer . . . was here too. Looking for the weapon he had used. Or she had used?

He looked at Alfreda. Not accusing you, but here you are,

and still hanging around. Still, you don't look like a killer. She had been saying something, not that he had listened. There you are, talking away. Attractive lady, I could fancy you under better circumstances and if I wasn't a more or less happily married man. Bit old for me, anyway. Watch it, Walker. You have a wife . . . and possibly more . . . but these home pregnancy tests didn't always get it right, did they?

'Must be connected with the other deaths,' went on Alfreda. 'She must have discovered something. Or have been about to.' Then she looked at Walker. 'Whoever did it might still be in the theatre . . .' Her voice dropped. 'Someone who works here . . . one of us.'

'Oh, shut up, Mother,' said Barney, 'you're just upsetting yourself. It's a public place, this theatre, wide open and you know it, anyone could come in. And go out . . . Anyone. Anyone could come in and walk away, this is a theatre, not a prison.' His eyes fell on Walker. 'A policeman as much as anyone else.'

'Barney,' warned his mother. 'Your tongue.'

'I speak with tongues . . . Only joking. Still, don't blame the theatre crowd when it could be anyone . . . There was a chap hanging around the dressing rooms before the show . . . seedy-looking chap, didn't like him, maybe it was him. Who knows?'

Walker was only half listening. He could hear sounds of arrival. Feet hurrying this way. First the ambulance team, then the men from the accompanying squad car.

And finally, running, Superintendent Phil Lewinder.

Walker had not personally told Lewinder but somehow he had got to know. And here he was, mark of a good copper. Walker said a prayer under his breath, hoping his own behaviour would escape criticism. He had done it all by the book, but sometimes the boss figures expected you to have read a different book.

And this was Stella Pinero, Mrs Coffin, lying here with the doctor already kneeling by her side, gently examining her.

Walker moved forward to speak to the superintendent: 'Sir – ' But Lewinder was too quick.

He was staring down at Stella. 'My God.'

113

'Sir,' Walker tried again.

Lewinder did not answer, he had gone white. He stared from Walker to Alfreda and then to Barney without really seeing them. 'Take these two away, put them in a room somewhere and ask them to wait.' Alfreda looked as if she was about to say something, then she thought better of it, and kept quiet. But she did not move, nor did Barney.

'Come on,' said Walker, touching her arm. 'Let's move.' He did not know where to take her but he would find somewhere. To add to his worry, he thought he could hear sounds of clapping and the performance ending.

'Get on with it,' muttered Lewinder.

Then he turned back to look at the doctor.

In the silence that followed, there was a murmur of consultation between the doctor and the paramedics from the ambulance as they began to lift Stella from the ground on to the stretcher.

As they moved her, a great gout of blood fell from her nose on to the ground. No one mopped the blood up, nor did they walk in it, they just stepped over it, the ignored blood.

Lewinder followed behind, leaving instructions to the CID detective who had just arrived to tape off the whole area and keep people out.

Walker turned towards Alfreda and Barney. 'All right, we're coming.' She did not sound pleased. 'We will wait in my office, it's down the corridor. The whole place will be swarming with people . . . the cast is coming offstage and the audience is out . . . they ought to have taken Stella out the stage door. Not the front as they seem to be doing.'

'It'll be the ambulance,' said Barney. 'Couldn't get an ambulance in there, it's very narrow and there are two cars parked in it as well.'

'Nothing to be done now,' said Walker. 'Show me where your office is.'

'I am frightened by all this,' said Alfreda, talking to no one in particular. 'Silly of me, I know, but there it is.'

'You talking to me?' Barney turned his head.

'No talk.' She motioned with her hand. 'This way. Forward, it is.'

Probably wise of you to be frightened, Walker decided, blood washes off on all around it. I shall probably come in for my share.

They walked down the corridor, and approached a short flight of open stairs. Walker first, Alfreda behind, and then Barney. Through a glass swing door they could see the ambulance, already driving away.

Been quick, thought Walker, and just as well. The audience was already emerging.

'Up the stairs,' said Alfreda, motioning to a short flight of a dozen or so steps on the right. 'My office. If we must wait, not that we can tell you anything.'

Barney interrupted, he was looking through the glass door. 'That man out there, the one leaning against the pillar and reading the programme . . . he's the one I saw hanging about, I told you about him. That's him.'

He stared at the man. 'And he's not really reading that programme, he's only pretending.'

In a flash, he was through the door and confronting the man. Then he stopped, puzzled. He knew the face, it was Harry, but Harry with a difference.

The man looked up, puzzled. Or that was what his expression said.

Alfreda ran after her son. 'Barney, please. Come back and don't interfere. This is not your business. Leave it to the police.'

But Barney's sense of drama had got the better of him. 'I am making a citizen's arrest. I accuse you of murder.' He put an armlock on his prey.

Walker came up and dragged Barney off his victim. If that was what he was.

He stopped, this was a face he knew, he had met this man. 'I know this man.' He pushed Barney aside. 'Harry . . . Harry Trent. Remember me? Bill Walker, we trained together at South Swinehouse.' Some years ago now, but he remembered the man, and hadn't he seen him around lately and wondered?

'What's going on?' Inspector Harry Trent picked up the theatre programme which he had dropped when Barney fell upon him. He held out a hand to Walker and muttered something about remembering him. 'I don't know what you are talking about.'

'It's him,' said Barney. 'Got to be him, I swear it.'

'There's been an . . . incident in the theatre . . . an attack on a woman.' Walker did not want to say more at that moment, he always had to remember Superintendent Lewinder, not to mention John Coffin.

Barney found his voice again. 'I saw you, I saw you hanging about the corridor where Stella was attacked.'

Harry Trent showed his shock. 'Stella? Are you talking about Stella Pinero?'

Barney was staring at him. 'It was you, it had to be you . . .' Then he faltered, his voice was no longer steady. 'But you've changed . . . You're the same, yet not the same.'

Harry Trent had the feeling he had often lately that another had taken over his body. He was the same and yet not the same, as if Merry had moved into him and become him. Perhaps they were not two people but one composite. No, rubbish, he told himself, trying to hang on to sanity. What sanity? He ran his hand over his face, trying to recover his identity.

'He has a twin brother,' said Alfreda.

Barney mouthed again, but to himself: the same, but not the same.

Which of us is which? Harry asked himself.

9

'I hate people who tread on me with heavy boots,' said Stella Pinero in a voice that started soft and grew loud – a shout.

'Hang on there,' said John Coffin, gripping her wrist.

'Boot,' said Stella. Then she tried again. 'Boots.'

'Yes, darling.'

'I don't believe in wickedness, it's all boots.'

'If you say so, love.' He took a tighter hold on her wrist, wanting to hang on to her in case she went away. She was not quite here, not absolutely in this world.

I wish she would give up on these boots, Coffin said inside himself, hardly formulating the words, and open her eyes.

'She may be confused,' the doctor had said. And so it seemed she was. He wanted his Stella back, this woman was a stranger.

He felt that if only she opened her eyes and looked at him directly, and not with an occasional glitter from beneath her lids, they would be in communication again.

There was silence in the small room with its white walls and long narrow window through which he got a glimpse of the tops of trees. The hospital, an old one, originally a workhouse, had been absorbed into the university and was now a teaching hospital. He released his wife's hand, she was quiet now, and went to the window. The dawn was coming up behind the trees.

There had been a lot of activity both from the medical staff and the police, which he had taken in automatically because that was his training, but which had seemed to be happening to another person.

I could read the report on it all, he admitted, but I don't

know if I would understand a word of it, no relation to me or my world.

At intervals during the night, nurses had come in to check the various wirings and drips that were attached to his wife. He had waited alone in a bleak little room on a lower floor while she was X-rayed, and operated upon. Her head was swathed in a turban of white bandages.

No real damage, a cheery young registrar had assured him, but one can't be sure with head injuries, in case of concussion, we just have to wait and see.

Which might just be his cautious way of handing over a parcel of bad news.

She's alive, though, the young man had added with some respect, as if that in itself was an achievement.

A Stella, brain-addled, who couldn't remember her lines, who could not perform, that Stella, he knew with certainty, would not wish to be alive.

Wouldn't be Stella.

He went back to the bed. Come back, Stella.

A nurse put her head round the door. 'Like a cup of tea?'

'Thank you.'

The tea when it came was hot and strong. On the saucer there was a little bag of sugar in case he should want it, thoughtful that, and a biscuit. He did not like sugar in tea and at the moment he felt that a biscuit would stick in his throat, but he recognized the kindness behind the biscuit, which was chocolate and rich. This was not a National Health Service – standard issue – biscuit but one from the nurse's private supply. Perhaps he ought to eat it just because of that. Can't look a biscuit horse in the mouth.

He knew he was rambling, not making sense. He drank the tea in several great gulps and felt better. For a moment his eyes had been off Stella's face.

Then he looked at her, and her eyes, big and blue, opened. They opened briefly, for a second, then closed again.

He leaned forward. 'Stella?' Her eyelids remained closed. 'Stella, darling. I love you . . . Say something, don't let me do all the talking. Say you know me.'

Slowly she opened her eyes again. Was she going to say

something to him? She licked her lips. Surely that was the preliminary to speech?

Even emerging from unconsciousness, badly beaten about the head, Stella was not the woman to say: Where am I? or What happened?

'I really stuck at it,' she said.

'I know you did, my darling, you always would,' Coffin answered. It must mean something to her, this comment from the deep, even if not to him. Or not at this moment. Perhaps she meant that she stuck at the survival game. And that, he hoped, was true.

Stella closed her eyes again, as if, having testified she was here and talking, no more need be said.

How much time passed, he was not sure, perhaps his own eyes closed, maybe he slept. Then she said, clearly and boldly: 'Is my nose broken?'

Coffin felt like crying. It was such a Stella remark. Of course, she wanted to know if her nose was broken, she was an actress, her looks mattered.

'No, darling,' he said tenderly. 'It got a blow, it bled badly.' It had looked an ominous sign of damage to the skull but the blood had come from a vein in the nose. 'You are a good bleeder, darling.'

Stella stared at him, then she said seriously: 'I fell on it?'

'I think so. It seemed to be what happened. There was a blow on your head, though.'

'He kicked me.'

'Quite right.'

First a blow on the head, the instrument as yet unknown. But by God, we will find it.

And then, or so the medics worked out with some help from the police, your body was kicked into the wardrobe and as far under the clothes hanging there as the kicker could manage.

That was how you got the worst of your injuries, but now you are awake and speaking, I know you are going to get better.

But I personally would like to kick the kicker from here to Land's End, but I will probably not get the chance.

'Tell me about my nose, my face.'

That was Stella, no doubt she was back in this world.

Or not quite. 'Write me a letter,' she said, and slipped away again.

To sleep, he hoped.

He pressed her hand, and fancied he got a slight pressure back. 'I'll come in later.'

He went home and slept, putting aside all his responsibilities to enjoy being a man whose wife was going to survive.

All the triumphs of his career which had given so much pleasure to him at the time seemed as nothing now, compared with Stella. His life had been a battle, with some defeats, a few retreats from the field, but on the whole a success. He was glad he had success, so that he could offer it to Stella.

Then he laughed at himself. Stella was the least sentimental of women and would not encourage such talk: she had her own victories to celebrate and did not need his.

When he returned, in the evening, showered, shaved and with a fresh shirt, he felt better and Stella was awake.

More, she was alert and sharp. Some of the tubes and wires which had impeded her had been removed and she was wearing a pretty blue bedjacket. On the way in, he had checked with the doctor and the word was very, very slight concussion but nothing to worry about.

She saw him looking at the bedjacket. 'Alfreda's been in, and she got this for me.'

'Oh.' He nodded.

'No, not one of hers . . . I always keep a few clothes in the theatre and this was there.'

'She's being very helpful.' He had written Alfreda down as helpful but this was a plus.

'Oh, Barney too, and May Renier, and as far as I know May hates me.'

'Oh, surely not? Why?'

'Oh, some man of hers, she thinks I ruined his career. Damon Horridge . . . he ruined it himself by drink, but she prefers to blame me.'

'I remember him, went to prison, didn't he?'

'He's out now and dropping poison in May's ear, I expect. Now you are here, I want to know what happened to me, and what you are going to do about it.' Definitely sharp. She probably had a headache and that always made Stella irritable. But she had a right to be so.

'I'm just enjoying seeing you so much better.' Obviously she had forgotten what he had told her. 'You were hit on the head,' he said, cautiously.

'I know that, I can feel it.'

He nodded. 'I don't know how much you remember . . .'

Stella frowned. 'I remember someone behind me, I remember the blow . . . I sort of remember . . . it's blurred, and I don't exactly remember being kicked, yet I think I was.'

'You were, or so the doctors think.' Hit on the head, kicked, and left for dead. Her attacker had surely hoped – believed – that she was dead.

Stella shifted uncomfortably in bed.

'I don't know how much you remember of what went on before . . . Why you were in the theatre or what you were doing near the wardrobe.'

Stella frowned and was silent. 'I came back for something . . .'

'We found your case,' he said. 'Nothing touched, papers in it, nothing touched.' Robbery was not the motive. A clever attacker might have made it look as if theft had been the motive, but this attacker had been in a hurry.

'I think I must have come back for that.'

'Do you remember anything of the time before that? When you came into my office? Do you remember finding the robe with blood on the sleeve?'

Stella still frowned. 'I think so . . . now you have reminded me . . . it's a bit distant. Funny how you remember things. I hope my memory is not done in for good.'

'It'll come back . . . there may be gaps, but you will probably remember everything . . . Why you came over here, who hit you?' There was a question in his voice which perhaps he should not have let rest there. Not the best of times to question her, really.

121

But he had underestimated his Stella.

'I was thinking of learning lines,' she said tartly.

She was better.

'What was I hit with?'

Coffin took a deep breath, he could see she was irritable and he did not blame her. 'There was a fire bucket down the corridor, full of sand and with a small axe in it, you were hit with that. No fingerprints,' he added regretfully. 'Or none of use. All blurred. Pity you didn't see anything.'

With asperity, Stella said: 'I wasn't looking for an attack. I don't know who hit me. A blank there. Sorry. Nor why.'

'We think that the robe that the killer used when he stabbed the Macintoshes had been hidden in the wardrobe, only you had already found it and, not knowing this, the killer came back for it and you were in the way.' We also think, or at least I do, that he or she didn't mind if you died too. Possibly wanted to kill you.

'How long was I lying there?'

'Not sure. If you went directly to the theatre after leaving me, then a couple of hours.'

'Who found me?'

'Sergeant Walker was sent over by Superintendent Lewinder to search the wardrobe for any blood; he found you. Alfreda and her son turned up as he did so.'

'I know, Alfreda told me. That's why she came to see me, she was upset, I think. I like Alfreda more and more.'

'I do too, if she's good to you.'

'A woman with a mission, but I am never sure what it is.'

She was talking above herself, it must be that blow on the head, loosening something.

'She's probably just trying to impress you. You are her employer, after all.'

'The Theatre Trust employs her.'

'It's you really, though. And you keep them all on very short contracts.'

'Have to. Money is tight.'

This conversation was probably not good for her but it seemed to roll on of its own volition.

'So who did it to me? Do you know? Have you caught him?'

Coffin was silent, debating what, if anything, to tell her.

'Oh, come on, I could see by Alfreda's face and the way she spoke that there was something, only she wouldn't say, and I couldn't get it out of her.'

Slowly he let the words out: 'Barney claims he saw Harry Trent in the theatre corridor earlier on.'

Stella thought about it. 'Harry? I can't believe he would attack me like that. And why should he? Have you asked him?'

'He was in the theatre, wanted to see the play again.' The words came out slowly. 'He has been questioned, and says he was just sitting there in his seat all the time. Can't get any witnesses to that, he may have been or may not as far as that goes . . . Only then Barney rather changed his mind. Said the man was like Harry, only different. Harry looking different.'

'His twin brother, then?'

Coffin shrugged, he didn't want to commit himself to what he believed. There were some aspects to the Harry–Merry syndrome that he did not care to consider. Might have to, though.

'You don't think so?'

'Not sure what I think.'

'What's happened to Harry?'

'He was questioned, he answered the questions and that's it so far.'

He could not help the note of doubt in his voice. Stella picked it up at once. 'But you aren't happy with it? Not satisfied?' She leaned back on her pillows, he could see she was tiring.

'I ought to go, not let you talk too much.' He looked towards the door. 'They will come bursting in any minute now and send me away with a flea in my ear.'

'You like Harry, don't you?'

'We go a long way back together. But I don't like everyone that I started out with. Far from it. One such tried to do me in, as you may remember. Harry and I were close, but not so very close. The years change things, I didn't know quite what to make of him this time round.' I was always that much older too. Sometimes it matters, at other times not. Now it does matter.

Quite a lot older too.

'You always see into people further than I do,' said Stella. 'I trust your judgement.'

'Thanks . . . not always right, my love. I make a mess like everyone else.'

'How do you judge people?'

'I don't know . . . by the feel of them, by experience, sometimes just by the look, or a combination of all three. You do a kind of deal with life and hope you get it right.' He had rarely been so frank with her on a professional matter. There was just a streak in Coffin of keeping women out of certain matters, although Stella was knocking it out of him. 'Harry felt right once.'

'And now?'

'He feels wrong.'

Stella looked out of the window, it was night, but the curtains were drawn back so that she could see the stars. There was no moon, it was a dark but clear night. 'Do policemen turn into killers?'

Coffin said: 'Some do. Perhaps we are killers, all of us, under the skin. Maybe it is why we take up the trade, we want to do it legally.'

'I thought he liked me.' Stella's voice was tentative.

'Did, does.' Harry liked women, that was something he knew about Harry from times past. Not that he was unique in that. 'We mustn't condemn him before we find him guilty. He may not be guilty.' He must get this right. 'Let me tell you about him. We worked together on a long case, I won't go into that, in a way it was a dull case, if important. I was climbing up the ladder, he was very junior.' He paused. 'I was doing a bit of drinking at the time.'

'Was I around?'

'No, hadn't seen you for a long time.' He smiled at her. 'Just as well, I wasn't at my best then, not someone you would have wanted. I got into a bit of trouble and talked my way out of it, he got into a work muddle – inexperience at bottom, and I helped him through it. Prop and cop. Trent and I just liked each other. Men can fall into friendship as well as into love. But it went with the job, I moved on, he moved on. We had the odd drink together. He got married, I got unmarried . . . Oh well, all of that part, you know.'

'There's always been a lot in your life I don't know about. Not that I mind.' Stella shook her head. 'Oh, I shouldn't have done that, it hurt.'

'You shouldn't mind, some of it you are better off not knowing. I realize that my mother and I have a lot in common, we bury the past and move on.' He looked thoughtful. 'Never actually killed anyone but I came close to it once or twice. And certainly wanted to.'

'We are back to policemen killing,' said Stella lightly, taking his hand. 'So what are you going to do about Harry Trent?'

'I'm thinking about it. Besides, it's not just up to me, there's Phil Lewinder and his team' – Coffin smiled – 'including Sergeant Walker, who seems to have fallen for Alfreda. Or is it for the boy?'

Stella said: 'Isn't Walker married?'

Coffin raised an eyebrow at her. 'Of course he is, but don't worry, I don't suppose he will do anything about it, and if he did, good luck to him. From all I hear his wife is a –'

'Don't say it.'

'I was only going to say that his wife is a career banker and earns about six times as much as Walker.'

'So where is Harry now?'

'Lewinder found him a room in that small hotel by the tube station, quite comfortable. He couldn't stay on at Alfreda's, but he can't leave until after the inquest on the other two.'

Stella looked in his face. 'You have made up your mind about something, haven't you? I can tell.'

Coffin did not deny it. 'I shall take Harry round on a tour to find his brother. It's the obvious thing, isn't it? Him and me, we will do it together.'

Stella gave him a long and thoughtful look before closing her eyes. 'You can go now, I'm tired.'

She kept her thoughts to herself, but had she expressed them then they would have been something on the lines of: Watch out, there might be more to Harry Trent than you think.

But after all, what did she know of her husband's mind? He was something of an enigma to her.

'Part of his attraction,' she said to herself firmly and loyally as she went to sleep.

As Coffin walked down the stairs from her room, he reflected that being in command meant there were times when you could do what you liked. And other times when you could do nothing.

This looked like a do-nothing time; because of his old friendship with Harry he ought to keep out of things and leave it to Lewinder. Not that he intended to follow that rule. No way.

At the bottom of the stairs he met the doctor who was treating Stella.

'How is she?'

'Doing splendidly, we will keep her here for another day or two just to be safe . . . With head injuries you don't want to take risks . . . and then she can go home.'

It was the new way with hospitals, reflected Coffin without surprise, in one day and out the next with no hanging about. Certainly the statistics for death in hospital must be substantially reduced by this arrangement: you went away and died quietly at home.

'Of course, we will be writing to her general practitioner,' said the doctor cheerily.

Coffin meditated on Stella's GP whom she rarely saw, since like most actresses she never admitted to being ill and would stagger on to the stage voiceless and crippled rather than let the understudy go on.

'Lovely lady, Miss Pinero. I'm one of her fans, she's promised me a ticket for her next show. I shall sit there

126

clapping like mad. The swelling on her nose will soon go down.'

'I think she was a bit worried about that.'

'Oh, she would be, but no permanent damage there. Well, on to work.'

Leaving the distributor of life and death behind him, Coffin drove home. He passed the Spinnergate tube station where Mimsie Marker kept her stall selling newspapers and cigarettes and condoms and absorbing in turn an extraordinary amount of gossip, some accurate, some false. She was one of Coffin's best suppliers of information.

However, she was not there now, her stall was packed up. Even Mimsie went home at some time, although she was always there about six in the morning. She was reputed to be one of the richest women in his bailiwick, with a daughter at a finishing school in Paris. Whether it was true or not, Coffin did not know, because, while knowing almost everyone else's secrets (including, no doubt, some of his), Mimsie kept her own.

Once in his tower apartment, he fed the cat and walked the dog; the cat came too. He was used to Stella being away, on tour or making contacts for new shows, but he missed her particularly tonight. The rooms were empty of life.

But there was one of her silk scarves tossed over the back of a chair, a book she had been reading was open on the table by the sofa, and he could smell her scent.

Before he could stop himself, he had picked up the scarf and buried his face in the soft, scented fabric.

Then he drew back to laugh at himself. Stella, the realist, would have said: Stop acting the fool. In the first place, I am not dead; in the second place, I am not about to die; and thirdly, the scarf does not belong to me but is one of your sister Letty's that she left behind.

Well, perhaps not the last comment, he was pretty sure that the scarf, gold and soft amber, was Stella's and certainly the scent (Guerlain's Mitsouko, she had trained him to know it) was hers.

He made himself a sandwich to fill this hole in his life, and while he was eating it, reflected that there was one thing he could do to deal with this hiatus in his life.

Lewinder first, and if he was in bed and asleep, bad luck to him.

But Phil Lewinder was awake and sounded alert, so Coffin gave him a good mark, while reflecting with simple cynicism that if there was anyone that the superintendent would try to be lively for it was his Chief Commander. There was a new Divisional post coming up soon and Lewinder was in the running.

'How's Mrs Coffin?' Lewinder got in first.

'Much better. Pretty well herself again.'

'Oh good, sir, very good. Glad to hear it.' He got pleasure and slight surprise into his voice, although he had cannily already made his own enquiry at the hospital.

'How are things going?'

'There will be a report on progress so far, might be there already, sir.' He went on slowly, as was his way, 'The blood on the floor outside the wardrobe all came from your wife, we knew that, but we had to make sure. On the other hand, the blood on the inner sleeve of the robe was of two types. These types match with the two dead people, as we are assuming that the stains came from the weapon or weapons used.'

'Looks as if the knife, if it was a knife, was tucked up the sleeve, hidden there.'

'Right, sir. My thoughts exactly. The forensic lab are pleased with themselves for getting a result so clear on a small amount of blood, but it wasn't mixed, if you see what I mean. A stain of one type on one part of the lining and another on the cuff. The killer must have withdrawn the knife and wiped it before using it again. Odd that, sir.'

'When we catch the killer we will ask why.'

'Even murderers have their ways; liked a clean knife, I daresay. If it *was* a knife – the shape is odd for a knife – not clear that, I am waiting for a judgement on that point.' He had almost made a joke there, but joking was not Lewinder's style. He had something more important to add. 'There were traces of blood on a small shelf at the back of the wardrobe, the shelf was loaded with old boxes of shoes, all shapes and sizes, presumably from former productions.'

Coffin fidgeted with the telephone. Get on with it, man.

'The guess is that the weapon, whatever it was, must have been hidden there. It looks that way. Scrapings of bloody wood have been taken and if forensics can get a result on that, then we shall be that much nearer. But my own feeling is that the weapon was there. The killer must have been on the point of collecting it when your wife got in the way.'

'You are still looking for it?'

Coffin could almost hear the frown that Lewinder was giving. 'Yes, sir. The theatre itself has been searched, and the grounds around it. The public garden across the road has had a quick going-over, and will get a more detailed treatment tomorrow morning. The trouble is that we are never far from the river or a canal here. But we'll go on looking. Once we've got the weapon, we've got the man, that's what I think.'

'Hmm, could be. So let's hope it's found.'

'It will be, sir.' Was there more certainty in Lewinder's voice than circumstances justified?

'What about the Macintosh house? Anything of help there?'

'Pretty negative, but I have a team still at it.'

Coffin said: 'Turn over the garden.'

'We've had a quick run over.'

'Try again and extend the search to the ground around.'

'Have been, sir. Made a beginning.'

'Try ferrets,' said Coffin, under his breath: Lewinder and his team could be very slow.

'Sir?'

Nothing. You didn't hear that.

But Lewinder wanted an answer. 'Are we looking for anything special, sir?'

'Anything that turns up. If it's important, you'll know it when you see it. Anything that relates to the other Macintoshes and their earlier life.' Prison, perhaps? 'Motive for their murder.'

Lewinder swore softly under his breath. 'And why no one reported them missing. A puzzle there.'

'I think so too.' Coffin thought: I mean you can die in one persona and live in another, and they may have done that, our first victims. But it was important, because those two were at the heart of it.

Lewinder was talking on, and had clearly said: Yes, sir, No, sir, while Coffin had been thinking.

'And I will be having another talk with Inspector Harry Trent tomorrow. I think that's justified, don't you, sir?'

Coffin said: 'Leave it, will you? I am going to talk to Harry Trent myself.'

There was a perceptible pause. 'Right, sir. Of course. You'll let me know if anything comes of it?'

'Of course.'

Coffin put the telephone down. So Lewinder did suspect Harry. And I believe that I do myself. But why, what have I got on my mind that signals his guilt? What is eating away inside me like a little animal with teeth. Sharp, insistent teeth.

It's this business with the twin brother. I never heard of the twin in the old days, nothing was ever said. I didn't know he existed until Harry turns up this time with the tale.

That's it: is it a tale, a fiction, an invention? Does he exist, this brother?

And if he does not exist, what on earth is Harry doing inventing a sibling. A sibling who is his mirror image.

That's what sticks in my throat. What a handy thing an identical twin could be. A wicked brother who looks like you but isn't you; who can do all the sinful things you might want to do but had better not. Not in your own person.

Why don't we all have someone like that to shove all guilt on to?

But, if this is what Harry has done, to carry it to such a length, he would have to be a very disturbed person.

Coffin got up and walked to the window where the night outside was calm and still. The killer must be a very disturbed person. Could there be two of them around the area of St Luke's Theatre at the same time?

He looked at his watch: the hour was late but not too late. He dialled the hotel in Spinnergate where Harry was staying.

After a pause, he got the reception desk, the voice that answered him sounded like the nightwatchman; it was not the smartest hotel in the world, but the man agreed to put him through.

A thick voice answered him. 'Who's that?'

'Coffin here . . . Are you awake, Harry?' Or drunk?

Somehow Harry cleared his voice. 'I am awake. Glad to hear you. I am sorry about Stella, a terrible thing to happen. How is she?'

'Better.'

'Thank goodness.' Harry sounded as if he meant it, but there was a wobble in his voice as if he was falling off a tightrope.

'Have you been drinking, Harry?'

'Only what you'd expect.' And how much was that these days, Coffin asked himself. 'And what about you, John?'

A sharp note there, Coffin thought, but fair enough considering his own past history. He ignored it. 'Well, lay off from now on, I want to see you tomorrow, and it'll be early.'

'Right. Doing what?'

'We'll be taking a walk.'

That silenced him. 'See you tomorrow. Have a good breakfast.'

'The condemned man, eh?'

Once again, Coffin did not answer. 'See you tomorrow.' As he put the telephone down, he was almost sure that the nightwatchman, so called, had been listening in. Must be a relation of Mimsie Marker. He might be worth employing for his information, except he was probably on someone's payroll already. Probably Lewinder's, because hadn't Lewinder fixed up for Harry Trent to stay here in the Beowulf Hotel?

He went to sleep thinking about the Beowulf Hotel and wondering how it matched up with the lodging house in Shambles Passage where Harry's brother had taken a room, only not used it too much according to Mother Arbatt's daughter.

*   *   *

131

He was woken in the morning by the cat, who, since Stella was an indulgent owner, kept no rules and answered to nothing and no one, but did what suited it.

'Push off, cat,' he said, removing her from his chest where she sat with solemn dignity and heavy weight. She was a cat with a history and a memory and knew that if you rested upon your owner and stared then food came soon. Why this process worked was no business of hers and she never thought about it, contenting herself with pursuing a successful policy.

Coffin got up, fed her and the dog, and made himself some coffee. On the whole he was glad to have been disturbed, because he had several things to do before going round to Beowulf's lair.

He drove to his office, determined to clear away some of the day's business before he saw Harry Trent. He needed a sharp view of the day ahead, and like a good housewife wanted his feet in the kitchen clear before he turned to the big problem.

Because it had to be faced: the killer of Joe and Josie, the pseudo-Macintoshes, was alive and around and had probably tried for him with a knife (his wrist still bore the mark) and had certainly gone for Stella. 'I ought to have held on to him and looked in his face, damn it. I am convinced this is the one killer of them all, I had him, and lost him.'

There was no one around in his office and so he could work on without interruption. He dictated answers to a clutch of letters, ready to be typed up when his secretary arrived; he made notes for a couple of meetings he was due to attend at which he would be required to speak, then stood up and stretched.

It was good to be alone here. His path in had been tracked and recorded, of course. He was not invisible and never could be. Nor, in truth, did he wish to be in the normal way. He would be lying if he did not admit that he liked the power of his position. He had taken years and much effort to get where he was.

But sometimes, as today, he wanted to be what he had been for years: a good detective. He left a recorded message saying that he would not be in further today. Then he departed in good spirits.

Yes, his car was watched as he drove away, and the word would go forth that WALKER was out.

He drove to the Beowulf Hotel where Harry was waiting for him. 'Had any breakfast?'

'No, I couldn't fancy any.'

'I couldn't either. Let's get some coffee.'

Harry looked around. The Beowulf appeared to be asleep for the day.

'There's a nice little coffee house near the tube station.' There was a theory that the real owner was Mimsie Marker, and it was certainly true that she breakfasted there as a rule. 'Opens early for workers. Well, we are all workers.' He was talking too much. 'Come on.'

'Are we driving?'

'No, walking. I've parked the car.'

They moved side by side along the pavement. Harry Trent spoke first: 'What's this about then?'

'Let's get some coffee inside us first.'

'I didn't bop Stella on the head if that's what's worrying you.'

'It's not just Stella, you know that.' Coffin marched forward. 'We'll talk, I promise that, but coffee first, then we walk.'

Wiggins' Breakfast Rooms had a dark brown antique air from outside but inside was clean and very warm and somewhat steamy. Early as it was, it was full of customers, quietly disposing of fried bacon and sausages which swam in a pool of fat.

They took their coffee into a side booth. The coffee was very hot and very strong, you could have cream with it if your blood systems could stand it.

Coffin took his black, but he noticed that Harry poured in cream and added sugar: nursery food for a man needing comfort. 'Like a bacon sandwich? They do good ones here.'

Harry shook his head. 'No, coffee will do. How come you know the place so well? Doesn't look like the sort of place you'd go for now.'

'You don't know much about me now, Harry.'

'No.' A long draught of creamy coffee went down his throat. 'I trusted you, John.'

'Let's leave trust out of it for the time being.'

'So what are we doing?'

'We're going for a walk.'

Harry looked at Coffin cautiously. 'You walk a lot, do you?'

'Sometimes, for a special reason. Like now. We are going on a manhunt.'

Harry sat back. 'You've changed since we worked together.'

'We all change.'

'But you've changed more. Not for the worse, I'm not saying that. But you have authority now and I feel it.'

'You change,' repeated Coffin.

Harry thought about that, then he answered it with a kind of cold sadness. 'I don't like the way you put that. I note it, don't think I don't take in the significance of the way you put it. I change, oh yes. I am not the old Harry all the time, that's what you are saying, isn't it? You don't know me always.' He added silently to himself: But I do not always know myself.

'I think I might not,' said Coffin carefully.

'So that is what the walk is in aid of?'

'You've got there at last. I wondered when you would ask. We are going to find your brother.'

10

It was a fine, dry morning when they had gone for their coffee, but by the time they walked out and bought the morning paper at Mimsie Marker's stall, it was clouding over with more than a suggestion of rain. Cold as well.

Coffin looked at the news headlines: war in the Balkans and trouble in the House of Commons over women's rights . . . shades of William Ewart Gladstone. History did repeat itself, but always with a difference.

He looked at Mimsie, who had handed him the paper, and saw before him the woman militant. Mimsie had fought upwards and owed nothing to any man. She was reputed to have this daughter, but the result of what coupling no one knew. It was hard to think of Mimsie in terms of virgin birth, but even harder to think of her with a lover.

'And how is Miss Pinero?'

Mimsie was always formal, even though she was capable of a leery light at the back of her eyes which gave him pause for thought on occasion. She acted as if she liked him, and he was grateful for her benevolence without choosing to examine its nature too closely.

'Recovering.' He was able to smile because an early telephone call to the hospital had confirmed it.

'Give her my best wishes,' said Mimsie solemnly. 'I've sent her some flowers. One of my favourite ladies. *The* favourite. I follow what she does. Of course, with my stall here, I can't go to the theatre as often as I would like.'

Seeing that she seemed to be on duty from dawn to well into the night, this was probably true. 'Of course you can't,' said Coffin soothingly.

'It's beginning to rain,' said Harry, putting his collar up.

'Won't be much,' Coffin said, not because he believed it, probably pour all day and soak them from head to foot, but because he was determined to go on.

Mimsie was interested. 'You out for a walk?'

'Working.' He had created this gap in his working life, it would not come again easily, and it must be used to dig up the truth of the deaths and lives of the Macintoshes. Harry knew more than he was saying, and feared it too. Fear was keeping him quiet.

Fear of what, though? Fear of his brother was Coffin's diagnosis. But like most diagnoses (including that still held over his own head, he mustn't forget that), it was yet to be confirmed.

Harry hunched his shoulders, he began to march forward.

'I'm afraid your friend is not happy,' said Mimsie in a loud whisper. 'I could lend you an umbrella.'

'No, thanks, Mimsie. It's stopping already.'

'So it is. We all have bad moods, don't we?' And she turned her eyes towards Harry, now standing waiting a few feet away. 'Especially him, but he's always been that way.'

Coffin let the words sink in. 'You know him?'

'Harry Trent, isn't it? He was a boy round here, he's changed but I always know a face.'

'Did you know his brother?'

A strange look passed over Mimsie's face. 'Was there a brother?'

'Twin brother.'

'Oh well, that explains it.' Mimsie went back to arranging her papers. 'Daresay I took one for the other. You would, wouldn't you? I expect they've grown apart now. As boys grow up, they do change.'

'Did you know the Macintoshes?'

'Not to say know,' said Mimsie as if weighing the matter up. 'No. Knew of.' She added: 'They didn't take a paper.' Clearly this put them in a subclass.

Coffin called out: 'Harry, come back here and talk to Mimsie. She remembers you.'

Harry hesitated, then turned towards them. Face to face

with Mimsie, he managed a smile. 'You remember me?'

'Delivered papers for me, didn't you? Years ago, as a kid, when you lived with the Macintoshes . . . Don't say you've forgotten.'

'No. Thought you might have, though.'

Hoped she had, speculated Coffin, keeping a watching eye on them both. What is it with you, Harry boy?

Mimsie was studying his face. 'I can see you as you were, now, the boy you were then. You were reliable, always did your round, fine or wet, hot or cold. More than you can say for some. Mind you, I don't say I'd have known you if it hadn't been for the Chief Commander here drawing my attention to you . . . You've put on weight, picked up a few lines, still got your hair.'

'Thanks,' said Harry.

'You used to make me laugh in those days . . . I'd think to myself, well, he's different today, proper little comedian. Other days, you'd be as sober as a judge. Wouldn't think you were the same boy.'

'And which boy did you like best?' asked Coffin.

'Oh, the sober one, to tell you the truth. I thought the jokey days had their cruel side . . . You don't mind me saying so?'

'I don't mind,' said Harry.

Is that what you say, nodded Coffin to himself. I doubt it. I don't think it pleased you at all.

Slowly, and as if it was a pain to say it, Harry said: 'I think you might have been confusing me with my brother.'

Mimsie put her head on one side and screwed up her eyes so that she looked like a lizard wearing lipstick (she liked a good colour) and rouge and a flowery hat.

'We spelled each other sometimes,' said Harry.

'Well, you do surprise me. But there you are, that's life. I ought to be past being surprised by now. What a funny boy you must have been. Two funny boys.' Her eyes were bright and shrewd.

Coffin wished he could read her mind. He imagined a tiny animal scurrying round inside Mimsie's head and picking up

137

interesting vibrations. Let's amplify that, he said to himself, what would I pick up?

Examine the nature of the twinship, she would be saying, and the twinship boys. I am not sure I know what to make of it.

Or were her brain waves telling the little animal that she did understand the nature of the twins, and he ought to watch out.

Coffin nodded at Mimsie (still engaged perhaps with that little animal in her head) and took Harry's arm.

'Let's get on. I want to take a look where the riot was and where you thought your brother might have been . . . it's some way off from here, so we will have to step out.'

Harry nodded. 'Swinehouse? I had a walk around there myself. All quiet and not too much damage that I could see.'

'Nasty while it lasted, though.'

'Sure, these skirmishes always are, you never know how bad it's going to get. You can take a bit of a beating while you are working that one out. But things seemed to quieten down very quickly.'

'There was a good team in charge in Swinehouse, it was all a bit puffed up anyway – I'm not sure how much genuine anger there was. And the girl started to recover quickly.'

'Thelma Birdways? She'll be out of hospital soon,' said Harry, striding forward.

Coffin raised an eyebrow, he was having a job keeping up with this energetic Harry. 'How did you know that?' It was true, he had been told so himself, having made the demand that he should be kept informed.

'Went to the hospital and asked.' Harry smiled. 'No, all right, don't worry. I didn't say I was one of yours. I just said I was a friend and wanted to know. I didn't see the child, of course, but yes, I was allowed to know she was on the mend.'

'What made you go?' They were well on their way to the district of Swinehouse; Coffin noticed with interest that his companion knew the way. He was leading them there.

'I like children. We haven't got any, can't have.'

'Kindly interest, was that the only interest?'

'You've got a sharp tongue when you like, John – no, I

thought I might find Merry there. Or see him. Or a trace of him. Faint hope, but I'm into faint hope. This walk is a faint hope, isn't it, but I'm here.'

'I know your twin has been hard to find. I have made a few enquiries myself and elusive is the word. What does he live on?'

'God knows. Me, sometimes. I do pass a bit of cash across.'

Coffin nodded. 'Well, you'd have to, wouldn't you?'

'What does that mean?'

'Just what it says. You are his twin. Twins are supposed to be very close, you wouldn't let him starve.'

'I sometimes think it wouldn't be a bad idea. Let him get thin and melt away.'

To his surprise, Coffin laughed. 'I know how you feel, I have felt like that myself on occasion. My sister can be a great pain, much as I have learned to love her, and as for my brother . . .' He didn't mention Stella, her shadow could never grow less in his life.

They were in Swinehouse by now, which was socially one step lower down than Spinnergate, and several from the richer area around the old St Luke's Church where Coffin lived.

They turned the corner into a short row of run-down shops which, although they were in need of paint and almost certainly in need of what builders call 'modernizing', were carrying on business. There was a butcher, a newsagent-cum-tobacconist, a hairdresser's, a pie-and-sausage shop (a type long gone everywhere else, but apparently doing good trade here), a betting shop, and a pub at the corner.

'The disturbance was in the road by the pub,' said Harry.

'You had a look there too?'

Harry did not answer. 'One or two of these shops got the windows knocked in, but I see they have been replaced.' He took another look. 'Not the betting shop, though.'

So you know which is the betting shop? You must have had a good look up and down Freda Street, that's the name, Freda. You couldn't tell from here that the dingy brown-painted building was where the locals went to place their bets.

'You can understand that,' said Coffin. 'It's always getting broken into. Probably boarded up all the time. Fancy a pie and sausage? They are open and frying, I can smell it.' So could most of the district probably, they didn't use good fat. Ancient fat, by the rancid stink of it, which had fried a sausage too many.

'No, thanks.'

'You could be right, might poison us. Still, we will drop in to ask if they have seen Merry.'

'It's not the sort of place that Merry would go in. I wonder it didn't burn down in the riot. It ought to have done.'

'I don't suppose that crowd were into promoting healthy eating.'

Outside the betting shop, two shops away from the pie-and-sausage establishment, Harry stopped, leaned against the wood protecting the window, to face Coffin.

'We're not getting anywhere, are we?'

'What do you mean?'

'We are looking for Merry because you think if it was not me who attacked Stella, and I am assuming you give me the benefit of any doubt there . . . No? Keeping an open mind? That's you, Coffin, no false sentiment . . . If it wasn't me, then it was Merry.'

Coffin said: 'I would like to see Merry, I don't question that you are right there. I thought that if we took this walk around together then I might pick up, one way and another, the sort of man he was . . . is.'

'Perhaps you think I have a doppelgänger. See, I know the word, I'm an educated man,' said Harry savagely.

And an angry one, Coffin thought, which, in a way, was what he had wanted to bring about. Anger does so loosen the tongue.

'You don't understand about twins . . . we are one egg split into two. Right hand, left hand. I am the right-handed man. He's the other side.'

'And there is a bond between you?' questioned Coffin. 'It's what people say of twins . . . a communion?' He was probing for something, and Harry was unsure what.

'We talk to each other like ordinary people,' said Harry,

140

his tone unfriendly, the relationship between the two men was deteriorating by the minute. Coffin was getting cooler while Harry was angrier. 'No telepathy or anything like that. I suppose we can make more accurate guesses about each other than ordinary siblings . . . that's all.'

'So it doesn't look as though you will be much use in finding Merry.' Coffin sounded a neutral note of regret.

'So we *are* looking for Merry?'

'I've already said so.'

'I am along then to sniff out the smell he may have left behind?'

Since this was not exactly true of why Coffin wanted him on the walk, his purpose being a little more devious, he did not answer.

His silence drove Harry on. 'You don't understand what it is like being a twin. You don't know what it is like to grow up always looking across the table at someone who looks like you. Your image, that's you sitting across the way from you.'

'A good feeling, I should think.'

'That's it: you don't understand. Sometimes it is good, you feel happy, because you like each other. Other times, it's bloody, you hate each other.'

Unstable pair, Coffin said to himself, swinging round and round. 'Does Merry feel the same . . . if you know, that is.'

'Of course I know. If I feel that way, then he must.'

Coffin nodded. Not so much unstable, he added, as unusual. Surely all twins were not like that? He remembered from his youth, while on a case in Oxford, meeting a pair of girl twins, one at St Hilda's and the other at St Hugh's who, if they happened to put on different dresses in the morning, went back and changed. They wanted to be like each other.

All the while, almost as if drawn by the smell, they had been quietly shuffling towards the pie-and-sausage shop. The smell was strong, and really no better the closer you got.

The door was open, showing a stone floor which was being washed down by a man with a mop.

'Not open yet, gents,' he said cheerily.

'You are open.'

141

'Not for serving. Just started frying, the fat's only just warming up.'

Coffin wondered from the smell if it had ever cooled down from the night before. It smelt like well-used, aged fat with quite a history behind it.

'Can we come in?'

'Oh Gawd, a copper.' The man stepped back. 'What is it now? We've been quiet since the last trouble and I wanted to stay that way.'

Coffin did not ask how he was known for a policeman, he knew he bore the stigmata. You came by it whether you wanted to or not: the way of speaking, the authority, even the way of walking. He had it, and so, to a lesser degree, had Harry. Did he preen himself or feel abashed? A mixture of the two, if he was honest.

The pieman soon wiped out that pride. 'Or you could be Social Security or Insurance, or one of those watchers.'

'Watchers?' asked Coffin, although he knew it was one of those questions better left unsaid.

'From the university . . . we got too many of them round here, two now and three by next year, that's where our money goes . . . they are always around asking questions and making surveys.' He looked at Coffin. 'No, no, your feet are wrong for that . . . they always wear trainers . . . jeans too, likely as not. No, after the troubles, you are bound to be here, you are police.'

'You had a bad time when there was the trouble? Bill Butcher, isn't it?'

Butcher nodded. 'That's me. I didn't personally, unless you count a day's takings lost because I had to shut up shop, but plenty were worse off.'

'I heard that you stayed open late because you were crowded with customers.'

'Oh well, when it was all over. Yes, I opened up again and we had one or two in.'

More than that number from all Coffin had gathered.

Butcher was giving him a careful look. 'I know who you are now . . . The big boss himself. Saw you marching once on parade on November the eleventh.'

Coffin nodded. 'You could have done.'

'I won't ask you what you are doing today . . . you wouldn't say . . . checking up on your friends and colleagues?'

'Quite right; I'm not answering.'

'That is an answer.' Butcher was polishing the counter while he spoke, his back to the sausages swimming in fat but still pale fawn in colour. 'Like a banger? Nearly done, I can smell. On the house, of course.'

'Not this time.'

Butcher flicked his eyes on to Harry Trent. 'Answer for both of you, do you? Can't he talk?' Then he leaned forward to peer into Trent's face. 'Wait a minute . . . you've had one of my sausages . . . you came in here the evening of the riots and had a plateful.'

'No,' said Trent. 'Your mistake. Never been in here.'

Butcher drew back. 'You look different, grant you that. Scruffier, you were . . . You one of those undercover boys?'

'No,' said Trent.

Butcher looked at Coffin. 'Well, you wouldn't say either, would you? Don't worry, I won't say a word. Your little secret is safe with me.'

'No secret,' said Coffin. 'Not mine, anyway.'

'I know he looks different, but it's the same man, cleaner and you have had your hair cut . . .' Butcher seemed puzzled but determined.

'I never eat sausages,' said Harry. 'I'm allergic to them, they make me sick.'

'You ate sausages that night.'

'If he says not,' said Coffin.

'I'll show you how I know' – Butcher reached forward, grabbed Harry's arm and exposed the wrist – 'look . . . see that scar?' It was long, and snake-like, but old, the wound which had caused it had long since healed. 'I saw that. Don't say there's two of you wearing it.' He turned back to his cooking. 'Just so you know I'm right.'

Coffin took Harry's arm. 'Come on, let's walk . . .'

*   *   *

143

The two walked on quietly for a while. 'Want to talk to any more locals?' asked Trent, breaking the silence. 'Or have you got what you wanted?'

A bit of both maybe, Coffin thought, a scrap.

'It wasn't me in the pie shop,' said Harry. 'So it must have been Merry. That's a sighting, isn't it? A smell of him, what you were hoping for. Although I don't know what it tells you, what the good of it is.'

'So what about the scar on your wrist.'

Harry walked on, head thrust forward. 'We both have one, twins are like that sometimes.'

'You mean it grew there out of sympathy?'

'No, that is not what I mean. I mean that when we were kids, Merry fell and tore his wrist on a rusty nail, he had a bad arm for weeks, it left a scar. I didn't have one, so I gave myself one. Now you know.'

Coffin looked at him with compassion. Good try, he thought, very good try. 'Merry got a passport?' he said.

Harry was thrown. 'I don't know . . . yes, he must have. Why?'

'Be on his passport, personal detail like that.'

'I don't have his passport,' said Harry. 'If he has one then he keeps it himself.' He hunched his shoulders against the rain which had begun to fall again.

They had reached the corner of the road and were turning into Russia Street which was narrow but widening at the northern end in a bulbous way so that the busy main road with buses and heavy traffic ran through it. No one liked Russia Street: it was not attractive, with its solid block of local government housing, but it was one of those streets you had to go through to get to the other side.

'To the west, is Pomeranian Street where Thelma Birdways lives,' said Coffin.

'Yeah.' Trent nodded. 'I know. I went to have a look, wondered if Merry might have gone there.'

'Had he?'

'Lost my nerve, didn't ask. But I left some flowers and a doll for the kid on the doorstep. Looked a comfortable little house. Well cared for, pretty curtains. A woman looked at me out of the window.'

144

A bunch of children were playing in the road. It was some nameless game involving a good deal of shouting. It did not look very childlike to Coffin somehow, but children in Russia Street had ways of their own. He had heard of them.

'Let's just take a walk around. Get the feel of the place. See what's going on. It's part of my job.'

'And is it one you do often?' I can't believe it, Harry's voice said.

'As a matter of fact, it is. My code name is WALKER.'

'Are you still looking for Merry? You want to find him before he does any more damage?'

'I'm keeping my eyes and ears open. You do the same.'

The children had moved nearer, staring at them as strangers. Strangers were noticed and not liked in Swinehouse.

They were a mixed group of boys and girls. Coffin counted heads quickly: eight, and a tall girl was probably the leader. She had that look.

They advanced towards the two men, forming a circle around them. 'Why aren't you at school?' asked Coffin. If there was aggression around, and he sensed there was, he believed in getting his blow in first.

'Have been,' said the girl. 'Prize day. No prizes for us.'

So they had not stayed. Coffin felt he could not blame them; he had been no angel himself at school, and there is nothing more boring and more irritating than watching the other people get prizes.

He nodded. 'Right.'

They were all fidgeting around on their trainer-shod feet, there was menace there, all right. Trent had moved slightly, just one pace behind Coffin.

'Don't like you, mister.'

'You're not obliged to, but I don't like you much either. Now move aside and let us get on.'

'You're a copper, seen you on the telly.'

Thank you for watching, Coffin thought, but did not say so.

'You can go, my dad says that for a copper you are straight . . . it's him we want.' She nodded towards Harry Trent. 'The one behind you. 'Cos we don't like him, we've seen him before and we don't like what we saw.'

'I have never seen you in my life,' said Harry.

From the back of the group, something soft and rotten was picked up from the gutter and flung at Harry; it hit him on the shoulder.

'Liar!' said Boss Girl. 'We know you even though you are dressed up so nice, but we'll dirty you down, you dirty pig.'

Coffin listened, he wanted to hear.

'The day of the trouble, we saw you, saw you on telly later on, too. Your face, all right. Perhaps you're one of those undercover policemen.'

There was a kind of howling that ran around the circle. Cats? Dogs or wolves? Not human and childlike but the more horrible for all of that. There was a phrase imbedded inside it, just heard: Get him, get him, get him.

'I know what you did to our Louie, that's why we want you. Took her round the corner and touched her up. You had a blue bike and you gave her a ride on it 'cos she can't walk very well, Louie can't, and you took her knickers off.' They were chanting knicker-picker as they surged around Harry Trent.

Harry stood still, as if waiting to be attacked. He flinched as something harder hit him on the head, and hands began to grasp at him.

Coffin moved in and grabbed the girl, the Boss Girl. She was tall and wiry but he was taller and stronger, he got an arm round and was moving her into the kerb. 'I want your name, and you can give me Louie's name and address while you are about it.'

'I ain't telling you nothing about me, but Louie lives in the Armout Buildings, Louie Best, and she's been ill ever since, poor little cow.'

There was a trickle of blood running down Harry's face, and he had the beginning of a black eye. His raincoat was half off his shoulders. He had stood his ground, but had not fought back. Coffin thought he was crying.

Coffin released the Boss Girl and moved towards him. But

as she did so a police patrol car roared towards them from the main road.

Boss Girl gave a shout: 'Run!' And ran herself.

Coffin and Trent faced each other. Trent was breathing heavily and mopping his face. 'I never saw any one of them and I never touched Louie, whoever Louie is.' He looked at Coffin with swollen eyes. 'It was Merry, it has to be Merry.'

'Well, we shall find out,' said Coffin as he walked towards the patrol car. 'Go into the pub and get some whisky. I will join you.'

In the pub, Harry had ordered whisky which he drank quickly. He was shaking and white.

The two men shared a booth, sitting on fake leather benches with a table between them. The place was not busy, only a few drinkers to eye them with covert interest. Got labels, we have, thought Coffin, they all know who we are. Probably watched the incident in the road.

'Poor Merry,' Trent said, 'doesn't seem as if he brought much joy around here, nor got much himself . . . Just pain all round . . . I wish I could find him, sort all this out.'

'So do I,' said Coffin; he was drinking tonic water.

'What happened with the patrol car?'

'I spoke to them, sent them away. They knew the big girl, she's well known, and I'm not surprised, she's called Dawn April, if you can believe it.' A well-known local liar, so there might be some hope there, but they would check on Louie and initiate whatever must be done. If anything, but he did not tell Harry this.

'My God, Merry . . . no, I can't believe it was Merry. I'd like to see him. Shall we try the house he was lodging in?'

'In Shambles Passage? No, I don't think so. I've been there myself and there's not much to gain from another visit. Unless you'd like to talk to the landlady?'

Harry shuddered visibly. 'No, thank you. I think I ought to tell you that I had a meeting with him one night, near the theatre.'

Coffin said: 'You should have told me before.'

'I didn't know what to do, I could hardly believe it was

him . . . he was changed. I remember thinking we aren't so alike any more, you've moved away. Of course, there was still a physical resemblance. Outsiders might not notice.'

'No,' agreed Coffin thoughtfully, 'they do seem to have difficulty in separating the two of you.'

'He told me he had a job with a haulage firm, that he was trying to make a new life for himself. I rang up a few firms, couldn't track him down.'

'If he was at one, then Lewinder's team will get on to him, and Jack Angus and Bea Kallen (she's a good detective) are still working on the street trouble; he might know something.'

Harry was looking less shaken. 'I'll go and wash my face.'

'A good idea.'

'I feel better now.'

'It upset you, though.'

'Of course. I can't bear to think that Merry . . . No, I won't think it.'

Coffin said: 'Go and tidy yourself and then we'll talk.' While Harry was away, he took a small, leather notebook, a present from Stella, out of his pocket. There was a pen attached which he used to make notes.

When Harry came and slid into the seat opposite, Coffin began to talk almost to himself.

'Leaving aside for the moment the matter of the child Louie, we have two murders, four dead people. And the name of Trent seems to come into all four. The Macintoshes, and the Trents, stuck together. They slip into position side by side, somehow, whether we like it or not. Then there's the attack on Stella, the name Trent comes in there too. You or Merry, but which?' He tried to keep his voice equable. 'I don't like it, Harry, but there it is.'

Harry nodded. 'I know. If it was me working on the case, I'd put me in the frame, all right.'

'The real Macintoshes, your Macintoshes, died a long while ago. Seems likely they were drugged, but there had been blows to the head in each case. Don't know more, at the moment.'

A noisy couple came in, man and woman, laughing

together. Coffin kept quiet until they had gone past to sit at the bar.

'The other couple, the pseudo-Macs, Joe and Josie, are beginning to give up a secret or two. They were show people, performers. Did a comic act together as the Two Macs, so it explains their use of the name, although in neither case was it the real name. Joe Flinters, and Jack Cash, seem to be the genuine names. They had been together in every sense for almost twenty years.' He looked at his notes. 'Got that information in a report from Lewinder before I came out this morning. Mean anything to you?'

Harry shook his head. 'Not a thing.'

'It's a beginning.

'We need to find your brother. If I can put it like this: Merry seems to put in an appearance and then pop away again.'

'So he does, so he does.'

Coffin said carefully: 'Was he always like that?'

Harry looked away. 'Just lately, yes, that's been the way of it.'

'I expect you can guess that a check is being made on Merry? To find out where he is, where he has been.'

And if he exists at all outside what might be your sick mind – Coffin allowed himself to think the dark thought at last.

You have the scar, Harry, you seem to have the right face. You have answers too, but are they the right answers?

He seemed to have talked himself out; he stood up. 'There's a phone over there, I'm just going to phone Stella and see how she is.' He looked at the clock, always fast, as pub clocks invariably are, but it was almost midday.

'Right.'

Stella, when he got through, was cheerful and alert. 'They are going to let me home tomorrow, if I promise to be good and stay in bed and rest.'

'And will you?'

'Yes, of course.' There was conviction in her voice, but you had to remember that she was an actress. Then she said, in

149

a considering way: 'Unless my agent rings me up with a too-good-to-miss offer.'

'Stella!'

'Ah, ah.' A ripple of laughter. 'Caught you. Of course I won't go dancing off.'

If he could only believe her. For a police officer, a detective of many years, trained and sophisticated, he was no match for Stella Pinero.

I'll show you, Madam, he thought, with a smile as he imagined exactly how he would show her. And then he remembered the secret he was keeping from her, that might postpone that consummation for some time.

When he got back, Harry was sitting, slumped, eyes closed. 'You sick?'

He opened his eyes. 'No, just thinking, seeing pictures . . . Will you do something with me? We are near the Dockland Railway, here?'

Coffin nodded. There was a station not far away.

'Come with me on it, then we can walk through the Greenwich tunnel and then to where I live. Not far.'

Coffin assessed the man's mood; he was dead serious, no doubt about it. 'Why?'

Harry looked at him, looked towards the ceiling. 'There must be something about Merry there.' He sounded vague.

Coffin stood up. 'Right you are. Let's get going.'

They took their tickets from the automatic machine, and waited for the crocodile of the train to appear. When it did so, the doors opened silently and they stepped in. The carriage was almost empty. Harry led the way to seats at the end of the carriage where no one was.

As the train rattled along on its narrow rail, Harry leaned forward. 'I want to talk.'

'Go ahead.'

'I want you with me when we get to the house . . . I think there may be a body there. Been there for a few days . . .'

Coffin said quietly: 'Your brother's body?'

'No. My wife's. I think I have murdered her.'

'Don't you know?'

150

Harry rubbed his hand across his head. 'Like a dream. I dream I did it. I ring her up and talk, but it's all pretend, she doesn't answer.' Into the silence, he went on: 'I know that if her body is there, you will see me right, help me do the right thing.'

'I will.' This is a seriously disturbed man, Coffin thought, and it's catching; I am beginning to feel disturbed myself.

'I'm a coward, you see, I might try to run away.'

'We all have that feeling,' said Coffin. 'Had it myself more than once. But yes, I'll keep you straight. But Harry, surely you know if you killed your wife or not?'

'I hit her, I know that. She hit me, for that matter. But now I wonder if she died as a result of what I did. I may have blacked it out. I keep having this picture of her slumped across the bed . . . Comes into my mind and I can't drive it out. If I killed her . . . I tell you the idea has been haunting me. I've got to make sure.'

He leaned back in his seat and waited for the journey to end.

Together, they walked through the Greenwich tunnel under the loop of the Thames. The tunnel was a monument to Victorian engineering, it had withstood the years and several wars, occasionally getting some redecoration but constantly in use. A gentle dampness suffused the walls, with the odd drip and trickle here and there, but you felt safe inside, the river was resisted.

They were silent as they walked, so silent that they could hear the sound of their feet echoing against the tired walls. The feeling of unreality inside Coffin grew stronger. But there was no going back. If Harry had murdered his wife, the sooner she was found the better.

'I suppose you have your house key with you?' he asked.

Harry patted his pocket like the best man at a wedding. 'Yes. I have it. Anyway, we keep a key hidden in the garage, so we can get in.'

Marvellous security for a policeman, Coffin did not say.

'Not far to walk once we're out of the tunnel. Across the main road, up Maze Hill, then a turn to the right. Heath Row . . . it's a row of newish houses. We were the second owners, not that I own it, mortgaged, of course. You've never been there, have you?' Harry had found his tongue and was carrying on now as if he had invited Coffin home to dinner.

'No, never been there. But I know Greenwich fairly well and I know where Heath Row is.'

He could imagine it too: the neat, pretty houses built a decade or so ago, with small front garden and a garage built into the house. Pretend Georgian or imitation Regency, Heath Row being near some charming genuine examples of such architecture. Altogether it sounded a more expensive bit of property than a serving detective inspector could be expected to own. Or mortgage, as Harry had pointed out.

'My wife inherited some money when her father died, she put it into the house. More her house than mine, really.' He added reflectively, 'What soured things between us, I suppose.'

Coffin reflected that Stella often earned sums much greater from her film work than any he came by, but equally she was capable of falling into debt, at which time, she was glad to have a steady earning husband around.

'Does your brother know the address?'

'Oh yes, he's never been there, though. We haven't been on calling terms for years.'

He may know where to find the key to the house, if it's a family trick, reflected Coffin.

'It's not likely then that we will find your brother sitting on your doorstep?'

'I wish he would be, but no, I don't see it happening.'

The bruise on Harry's eye was coming up nicely, a blue stain appearing through the red. 'Bit of a headache,' said Harry, touching his eye.

'Not surprised.' An accusation of child abuse, the threat of two murder charges hanging over you, not to mention that you might be accused of attacking the Chief Commander's wife, would give anyone a headache.

And brother Merry, the disappearing twin.

The hill was as steep as he remembered but Harry strode ahead, setting the pace now. Halfway up, they passed a postman, pushing his bike and fumbling with his sack of letters.

He looked up: 'Hello, Mr Trent, got some letters for you. Want them now?' He gave a hearty guffaw as if he had said something funny.

Well, that's one that got your name right, Coffin thought without humour; he did not join in the laugh. Jokes were hard to appreciate just now.

'Please.' Harry held out his hand to receive two brown envelopes, clearly bills, and a picture postcard. He looked at the picture. 'Tower of London.' He turned it over, then said, without surprise: 'It's from Merry.'

'What does he say?'

'Not much. Here, have a look.'

The message was scribbled in clear but pale writing: *Harry, sorry not to have seen you again. Let's meet. You know where I am. We must join up again, let's get ourselves together. Merry.*

'Recognize the writing?' The staggered print could have been by anyone.

'It's signed. Yes, that's how Merry wrote. As far as I remember.'

'Do you know where he is?'

'Only the house in Swinehouse, don't have another address.'

Where he hasn't been seen lately, thought Coffin. Lovely day this is being. And I haven't got much of my free time left. How would I have reacted if the postie had said: Just saw you walking up the hill, Mr Trent, thought you had passed me.

Would I, John Coffin, rationalist, have to believe in a doppelgänger? Or would I have settled for brother Merry?

But it had not happened, there was a card instead, which Harry put in his pocket as they strode on.

'Often send you a card, does he?' he panted, as Heath Row came in sight, with a glimpse of the heath itself beyond it.

'No, never. Not on birthdays, not at Christmas . . . But then I don't write either. Rings up when he wants something or he's in trouble. I expect you think I am stupid to worry over him, but I can't help it. He's part of me.'

Coffin nodded. 'Yes, I realize that.'

'Well, I'm the one in trouble now.'

153

'Ought to bring him out of hiding,' said Coffin.

Slowly, Harry said: 'Do you know, I believe it might do.'

'Face to face.'

'I don't know about that, we hardly need that seeing we've only got one case of features between us . . . joke.' Neither man was laughing. 'Here we are.'

He pushed the gate made of fretted iron painted black. The house was much as Coffin had imagined it with a solid white front door with a brass knocker in the shape of a fish. On either side of the door was a shallow bow window, the same above. Mock Regency, then.

The garage was separate from the house with a narrow passage leading to the garden. Coffin glanced at it briefly, taking in that there was some obstruction but turning aside as he heard Harry swear. 'Damn it, damn it.'

Harry was fumbling with the key, which he dropped. His hands were shaking, and a tremble shook his shoulders, neck and head.

Coffin bent down. 'Here, let me.' He had the door open, pushing it aside to let Harry go in. 'You first.' And then, when the man hesitated, 'Come on, get it over.'

He gave him a push over the threshold, then followed him in himself, sniffing the air.

There was no smell of death.

The small hall which was covered in cream paper had a staircase leading up from it and a door on the right through which he could see the kitchen. There was no furniture in the hall except a table with a pot plant on it. The plant was certainly dying, from neglect by the look of it. He touched the soil which was bone dry.

'Kitchen, sitting room or upstairs?' he asked Harry. 'And better shut the front door behind you.'

Harry hesitated, then he walked slowly up the stairs towards the bedroom.

Coffin waited, then went up a few stairs, stopped to listen, then moved.

When he got to the landing, Harry rushed out of the

bedroom, ran into the bathroom where Coffin could hear him being sick.

'So what did you do?' asked Stella. She was out of her hospital bed, wearing a dressing gown which Alfreda had brought in for her; she was setting herself out to be entertaining for her husband, whose mood seemed overtense.

'I made him some tea, got him some whisky, and made him lie down. He went to sleep, so I left a note and departed.'

'He must have been exhausted.'

'By emotion. I wasn't sure whether he was overjoyed that he hadn't killed his wife, or disappointed.'

'You don't mean that.'

'No, I suppose I don't.' There were enough complications around without a wife killing. 'She's cleared off, though. I had a look round the house and I would say she had taken most of her clothes. I didn't tell him that.' There were some things it was better for a man to find out on his own.

'I feel sorry for him.'

'He's got some questions to answer.'

A thought occurred to Stella. 'You don't suppose she is dead and he buried her in the garden.'

'No, my love, trust my judgement. In the first place, I had a look round and no one has put a spade to that garden for weeks. It's a mess but an unspoiled one. And there is no attic, and nor is she under the floorboards – they have rugs on a polished floor and it would have showed up.'

'Ah.'

'Yes, ah. Also, she left a note. It was in the kitchen where I left it for him to find.' He had not read it but he could guess the contents. Harry's wife, as he remembered her, was not a woman of great originality of mind, and her words of farewell would be the usual formula. 'Not happy', and 'but I wish you well', and 'we must stay friends.'

Not much chance of that, Coffin thought, because the future for Harry was rocky indeed.

'Did you come back on the Dockland Railway?'

'No, I'd had enough of that for the day. I walked down to that little restaurant you and I have been to once or twice,

155

and had a cup of coffee. I rang for a car to collect me.'

'That was sensible.'

'I wanted to think. About you, my love, among other things.' He reached out to take her hand. 'I'm glad you are better. Home tomorrow? I'll come for you.'

'Not with all you have on hand. Alfreda will come.'

'Me, and no one else.' He tightened his grip on her hand. 'I don't think you know how I value you.'

Stella smiled, her eyes full of affection. 'I am not going to pack up and run away.'

He bent over to kiss her cheek. He was not lavish with kisses, they meant more to him than the casual endearments of her stage friends.

'Darling creature. How are the animals?'

'Oh God, they never stop eating. But I am getting short of their food, I had a shopping list, and they were on it, but I forgot.' Eased out by Harry Trent, by his twin brother, by the double murders in his territory with the press racing round.

'What a mess it is.' He went to the window to stare out at his Second City below.

He had not told her that when he left the house in bloody Heath Row, he had looked down the narrow passage between house and garage to see a bright blue bicycle parked there.

11

Jekyll and Hyde were coming together, joining up, fusing, and it was painful for both parties. The pain was shared equally between both. They were beginning to talk to each other now with the same voice, turn and turn about.

The truth was that they did not like each other, were ashamed, one of the other. Feared each other, even. And were right to do so because life for one was death for the other.

Perhaps this had not been understood clearly at the first surfacing, face to face. (If you could call it so.)

'Am I body or mind?' asked Hyde. Of the two, Hyde was the intellectual while infinitely the more driven, the nastier. More full of hate, more apt to fall into violence. Not always rational violence, either. It was apt to spring out of Hyde like a tiger as if it had a life of its own. Death was very close to Hyde.

Jekyll had a conscience, he had the conscience for them both, since you cannot have both a conscience and a tiger inside you. He felt the weight of Hyde's activities which, for a long while, he had been able to pretend were nothing to do with him. In his heart, however, he knew otherwise. 'We are in this together,' he said to Hyde. 'Stuck with each other. I have to bear your guilt.'

That was the pain, because Hyde found he had to bear Jekyll's pain as well as his own. Not that there was much of that, but it hardly mattered since Jekyll had plenty to spare. 'Hold your tongue,' he wanted to say. 'Get out of my way, let me be all.'

A conversation between two persons, one of whom is necessarily mute while the other speaks, is not easy.

But there are always dreams. Daydreams, waking dreams, through which the other voice can speak.

Each knew that oblivion was approaching. But which would die?

One creature with two heads, one head had to go. Or, think of it this way, two heads caught in one body. Surely, death was kinder?

But there was nothing kind or gentle in the fate laid out for Jekyll—Hyde, it had been earned and would be delivered.

12

A heavy curtain of rain fell that night, turning everything grey and sombre. The gutters ran with water, the pavements shone with puddles, and rainbows hung around the street-lamps. A mood-changing night.

Coffin went back to his solitary home, happy that Stella would soon be with him, but more troubled than he had expected to be about Harry Trent. He was puzzled, and worried.

He fed the animals, gave himself a strong drink and considered telephoning Harry. Say to him: Now what about this scar on your hand, and the blue bicycle. You and Merry both? What is it all about? A trance, a dream, is that what you have fallen into? And by the way, there is a letter in the kitchen from your wife, she is probably saying goodbye.

No, better let him sleep.

One telephone call, however, he must make.

Superintendent Phil Lewinder, whom Coffin was coming to see as the sole voice of reason in this case, largely because he was a quiet man who spoke but little, received, as was no more than his due, a summary from Coffin of his hours with Harry Trent. He took it quietly, without showing resentment at any interference in the case of the Chief Commander. He was an able politician and knew that Coffin had much patronage at his command, and there were several positions coming up that he was interested in.

It was late evening when Coffin spoke to him on the telephone but he took this in his stride also, although he had been quietly reading in bed, enjoying the splash of rain on the window. He was a man who worked on his comfort, giving his arrangements thought, thus his pillows were soft and yet not too supportive, but they propped up a heavy man sitting to read. His house had large, well-upholstered chairs on thick carpets. The house itself was unpretentious but solid, with everything in it from lavatory to deep freeze, the best he could afford. He was a Man of Property.

After talking to Coffin, comfort gone for a while, he got up and paced about the house, much to the irritation of his large and comely wife, who frequently acted as his voice on issues where he remained silent.

'What are you doing, Phil?' She too was reading in bed, the latest from Joanna Trollope, and she had not wished to be disturbed.

'Thinking, dear, about what the Chief had to say.'

'You shouldn't let him bully you.'

He ignored that, and went back to remembering the conversation. He was not happy at the investigation into what the papers were calling 'the double Mac murders'. Not much progress was being made. They still had not found the murder weapon for Joe and Josie. The postmortem on the long-dead other victims was beginning to suggest that a sedative as well as a blow to the head had been the means of death in both cases.

The man who had performed the autopsy was an energetic young man full of ambition. He had groaned when Lewinder, urged on by Coffin, had pressed him for a judgement on the length of time the bodies had been in the ground.

Carefully, Dr Archer explained that his was not an exact art in spite of what the lay mind thought. 'After a certain time it is hard to be precise.' Soil quality, damp, and so many other factors came in, he explained.

'I don't want day and month,' said Lewinder, 'although it would be helpful.' He looked hopefully at Dr Archer.

Archer pursed his lips, a scholarly habit he was practising with a view to television appearances. 'Let me say between five and ten years.'

'Oh, lovely,' said Lewinder in a sour voice.

'I can narrow it down a bit: the woman had vomited on

her dress, so there were traces of food debris on the fabric. That was where the traces of drugs were found, a sedative, marketed under various names. The way the chemicals had broken down suggests the figure of five years is the better of the two. The best I can do.'

It was all Lewinder got from him.

He went back to his own small team which he had set up to make the nucleus of the investigation. Mobile telephone, and pagers, kept them in touch. Lewinder was grateful for modern equipment but he sometimes longed for a large force of detectives plodding round on foot. At the heart of his contact group was a woman detective who managed faxes and green screens flashing with messages. You always had to hope, he told himself, that she kept her eyes on the screen.

He needed a bigger team of detectives, he told himself, he was being starved of help.

He was thus both grateful and yet suspicious of any help the Chief Commander could give him. A brilliant detective with a marvellous track record. Yes, once. But ought he not to be concentrating on getting more funds for people like Phil Lewinder himself?

'I will check on Trent myself tomorrow,' Coffin had said, his voice polite but brooking no argument, 'he was asleep when I left. I don't know where he fits in, nor where his brother does, but they are in there somewhere.' Coffin did not cross his fingers as he mentioned Merry, but had he been a superstitious man, he might have done so. 'Get in touch with Trent's chief in Greenwich, and find out what his mental condition is: I know he had an injury, I guess he needs help.'

'Will do,' promised Lewinder. He could see his outfit was going to be stretched. Could he ask for more men?

'And I would like you to send a man round tonight, to check on a blue bike tucked away at the side of the house. I suggest he puts a padlock on it; anyway, see that it can't be removed. Trent can be questioned about it in the morning . . . You mean to see him?'

'I do, sir.' The sir came out as an afterthought, because his mind was already running ahead to that interview, trying to

161

assess the new information and relate it to Inspector Harry Trent, CID officer from another outfit, but of whom he had heard. 'I need to talk to him again about the attack on your wife. The boy Barney sticks to his identification.'

'What about his mother? She was there.'

'More cagey. Not sure. She might have more to give, I think she might, but we will see. There's Miss Renier . . . she was just down the corridor, she says she saw him too, but she was further off.'

'I didn't know May Renier was there.'

'She came forward this morning to say so. I don't know what to make of her as a witness . . . I think she is telling the truth, she saw Trent, thinks she did, but I feel as though she is keeping something back.' But he often did feel that when questioning a witness, yet it was not always confirmed by later events. He frowned. Coffin could feel the frown and the puckering of the lips that went with it. 'She's a local woman, I know that, I think she was at the same school as my daughter, years older though. I know the headmistress and I might get something there.'

And he was picking up some more information about both sets of Macintoshes, the burden of which was that they could not be more different: the earlier Macintoshes being extremely strait-laced, whereas the Joe and Josie pair had been open minded about behaviour, although generally thought to be a friendly and decent couple. Fundamentally decent, the phrase had been, which to his experienced ears meant that there was something in their background that needed understanding. He had a sensitive ear for that sort of thing, you developed it in this job or you didn't get on. Trouble had a smell.

What was the official, police view of the double murders?

They were guessing that the two sets of killings were related on the general grounds of not believing in coincidences (although they did happen). The motive for the killings was as yet unknown.

'Won't find out till we get the killer – if we do get him, or her – that's my guess,' thought a gloomy Lewinder whom the late night was not suiting.

The attack on Stella Pinero was probably because the weapon had been hidden among the clothes in the wardrobe and she might have found it.

'Although *we* didn't.' Another sour thought.

But what it showed was that the killer was nervous and knew his or her way around the theatre.

So, to the picture of a skilful killer with no known motive, they could add the fact that he was one who knew his way around the theatre.

In theory that would rule out Harry Trent, except for the evidence of Barney. And possibly his mother, and perhaps May Renier.

Tomorrow, he would interview Harry Trent, and then he would share all his thoughts with the Chief Commander. He had to hope it would be a two-way traffic. Meanwhile, he had sent off a detective to padlock a blue bike. It had been done, by a quiet call from downstairs.

Sitting in the armchair in the living room, he drifted off to sleep. He was awoken in the wet dawn by his wife bringing him a cup of tea and a sermon about not coming to bed.

His first thought, as he awoke, was: check if Trent has a brother at all.

John Coffin slept heavily, no dreams, and inside him the happy thought that tomorrow his Stella would be home. It had taken this attack on her to make him realize fully how much he loved and valued her.

Without her, the house was empty. Before sleeping, he had gone to finger the silk robe hanging on her dressing room door, then he had picked up one of the scent bottles on the table by the big, lighted looking glass (she was always a woman of the theatre), and rubbed some of the scent on the back of his hand. Rose and jasmine and a deeper, spicier background note met him, it was as if Stella was in the room but had withdrawn to a corner where he could not see her. He knew now that he could not survive without her. Or, he would live on, one did not die so easily, but the man inside him would be someone else.

That was the downside of loving someone: you paid. Or

was it more than that? A necessary wound, one's stigmata?

'I could kill the person who attacked you, even if there was no wound,' he had thought, as the scent lingered in the air, 'but because I am a so-called civilized man, I won't do that, but on my oath, I'll get him.'

It would be very easy to declare Harry Trent guilty and punish him, he was almost asking for it, but there was an impediment to rough justice: if Harry Trent was as gravely disturbed as he seemed, throwing up an imaginary twin, then you could not beat up a sick man.

'Don't remember hearing about this brother before,' he thought, on waking, unconsciously imitating Phil Lewinder. Not so very surprising, he thought, stumbling about the kitchen to make coffee. I never talked about my family, never mentioned my mother, and I didn't know about Letty and William in Edinburgh then. Not sure if I quite believe in William as a person yet. Can such a prudent fellow really be related to me and Letty?

But he had the evidence of his mother's diaries to tell otherwise. Mind you, Mother was a liar, a fantasist of surpassing skill. Which brought his mind back to Harry Trent and his twin.

Mother, apostrophized Coffin, as he drank some coffee, promise me that you have not created a twin for me?

He drank his coffee standing up, eating a stale biscuit with honey on it. Honey was for energy, he needed energy, and the staleness was for laziness.

The telephone at his elbow rang to interrupt him. He looked at the clock on the kitchen wall which said it was not even eight o'clock.

'Hello?' The call was from his doctor, an agile young GP called Keith, who was famous for starting work early so that he could get in a round of golf later in the day. Or so his patients said. 'Just to remind you that the results from your tests you were nagging about will be in at last so I have made an appointment for you to come in.'

'Oh, any idea of what the judgement is?'

'Wednesday is the day.'

'Does that mean the news is bad and you want to warn me?'

'It means I don't know.' Keith Foster was giving nothing away. 'Nine sharp. Can you make it?'

'Yes,' said Coffin dolefully. One more bloody inspection.

'Well, you needn't bother to come.'

'You know I will, but I'm not looking forward to it. You sure you don't know already and aren't saying?'

'You are a coward.'

'I am,' he sighed. 'But I will be there.' He had trained himself, like a good soldier, to keep his head down but move forward and face the guns.

One of the guns in this case would be aimed by Stella who would want to know what was going on and why he looked like that? He would probably not tell her then. Later, of course, she would know all about it, good or bad.

Damn, he thought. I ought to give all my attention to the Force I command, but I am sharing out what brain power the years have left me between the Macintosh murders and Harry Trent.

With a look in for Stella.

'Wait a minute,' he said to Dr Keith Foster, man of many interests, one of which was psychology, which included managing his patients. He was a short, red-haired young man, who usually wore jeans and an open shirt, but for the sacred game of golf he had an ancient tweed suit with bloomers which had belonged to his father and which did not fit but had undeniable style. Coffin thought it had probably belonged to the grandfather and was therefore an heirloom. Coffin did not play golf but sometimes shared a drink in the club with Foster. 'What do you know about twins and telepathy?'

'There have been one or two studies, more, probably, than the subject deserves. One in the States, a couple over here, and one in France, I believe.'

'Nothing in it, then?'

'I would say not much. That is the general consensus of opinion. Nothing more than you might expect between any pair of close relations: mother and child, husband and wife. Why?'

'Just a case I am interested in,' said Coffin. He thought for a moment. 'Tell me, could a person split off another person altogether?'

'There are many cases of multiple personalities, some quite famous and well written up. It's an hysterical phenomenon, although it may indicate more serious trouble.'

'And would, let's say Person A be aware of Person B and feel quite separate? Almost as if he was watching a play with a plot he did not write.'

'Consciousness is a strange affair, I can't lay down rules, I'm no expert.'

'And supposing this person – '

'Nameless, of course,' interrupted the doctor.

'Nameless,' agreed Coffin. 'Supposing this person thought he had killed his wife. But there were no signs of her death and I think she has just packed and left . . .'

'Then I should ask serious questions about this person's motive for doing all this. But motives are your business.'

'Quite true . . . motives are for me to discover. If I can.' He hoped he would have some good ideas on the subject before he turned up for the result of those tests. Suddenly he felt optimistic. 'Thanks, you've been helpful. Come and have a drink and a meal sometime, Stella would be pleased.' Keith was not Stella's GP (she moved around, having once preferred an elderly lady of advanced views on sex, contraception, abortion and women clergy, and then removed herself to a charming Indian into psychotherapy), but she found Keith attractive.

'Right, I'll come with pleasure. I would like to meet this anonymous figure you've been talking about.'

'You might one day.'

The apartment had to be readied for Stella's return. The couple employed a young woman called Ellen who very often brought her young daughter to work with her. Stella, who was practical about such matters, had given the child a toy vacuum cleaner, which worked, a miniature brush and pan, a duster with her name on and had offered a small wage. 'If she's going to come, she might as well do something sensible,' Stella had said. 'Keeps mother and child happy.' Coffin had to admit that this seemed to be the case.

He waited that morning for the pair to arrive, which they duly did, punctual as always. Punctuality was a virtue in Ellen which he appreciated.

He suspected that Ellen was an actress *manqué* and that she was planning a theatrical career for her poppet.

'So glad that Miss Pinero will be back.'

Coffin had not told Ellen that his wife would be home from hospital but she knew. He was not surprised, he had noticed in the past that the woman's information service was excellent. It made her one of those people he could make use of in the Second City Police Force. She always called his wife Miss Pinero which confirmed his suspicion that she was a thwarted thespian.

'Shall I make a casserole so there is some food ready?'

'Good idea.' Ellen was a tasty cook.

'I thought you'd say that; we did the shopping on the way here, didn't we, poppet?'

Poppet smiled without a word. She had a charming smile and big blue eyes. Coffin felt sure she would have a good career as a performer. In his opinion she was a performer already. Born that way.

'Chicken,' she said, flashing a smile on which orthodontics had already been at work, in Coffin's view.

'Good, chicken will be fine. Feed the animals, will you, please, Ellen?' Both the animals were devoted to Ellen because she fed with a lavish hand. 'I will be bringing Miss Pinero home myself.' When talking to Ellen, he found himself also calling his wife Miss Pinero.

He drove to work, happy in the thought that he would soon see Stella and that her bedroom would be garnished and polished to receive her.

I will telephone Harry, see how he is, and say to him: What is this about you and this brother you claim to have, that you both have identical scars and both have blue bicycles. I want a straight answer, Harry, even if it sends you over the top.

He was not surprised to hear from his secretary that Superintendent Lewinder had telephoned to ask if he could call.

'Yes.' Coffin looked at the clock. It was still early, but he wanted to be free to go for Stella later in the morning. 'Ask him to come. Now, if he can.' Why must he call, and why make a telephone call of it?

Lewinder must have been waiting, because he was being ushered in before Coffin had had time to read more than a couple of the reports and requests that always lay on his desk.

Coffin soon discovered why Lewinder wanted to call: he had a fancy to see Coffin's face as he delivered what he had to pass on.

'I spoke to Superintendent Bruce, he heads the CID team, knows Harry Trent well, naturally, although he says no one knows the man *really* well. Except perhaps Chief Inspector Ferguson – they are pals – but even he says you don't get close. He confirmed that there had been a recent injury during a raid and that Harry was on sick leave. Bad reaction, it seemed.'

Coffin nodded. It happened. You did not always come through unscathed, and it did not reflect badly on you, not in his judgement.

'But the blue bike, sir ... when DC Deller went to see what he could do, he found nothing. No blue bike, sir.'

Lewinder's eyes rested thoughtfully on Coffin.

13

Although Stella was laid up, the work of the theatre had to go on. Alfreda, as general manager, was very busy, while Barney was convinced he was essential to the smooth running of the theatre. May Renier, in charge of wardrobe, naturally had the same idea.

The two women were not friends: May Renier, a short, stocky woman, was envious of Alfreda's long-legged elegance, but there may have been other reasons; however, they worked well together because that was business and both valued their position in the theatre pantomime.

Alfreda had her own office, while May held sway over the wardrobe room, which was filled with the clothes for productions past, those still running, such as the *Oh What a Lovely War* uniforms, guns and all, and those in rehearsal, like the Priestley revival of *Time and the Conways*, hanging on racks, and with the designer drawings for those being made at the moment. She was assisted by Debbie and a sad-faced man called Dods who sat at a long white table cutting and sewing, all the while complaining gently about the ignorance of designers on what you could and could not create and, above all, what the human body could wear and move in. Around the room were stacks of big boxes in which were kept buttons, furs, coloured tights in all sizes and shapes, shoes and fake jewellery. One box said: Crowns, large and small. Next to it was another box labelled: Furs, for Shakespeare and Coronations. It was filled with soft, gentle fur called ginette which moulted all the time. This fur had been a bequest from a rich, dead actress.

May had borrowed a swatch of the ginette once to go out

to dinner with a new young man and he had sneezed all the time: the evening had not been a success. May had plans to use the fur for the robes of an eminent Shakespearean actor whom she disliked when he next brought Macbeth into the theatre. With any luck she might kill him. Such did her thoughts run. Perhaps everyone was thinking about death just then in the Stella Pinero Theatre.

Not to be mentioned to Miss Pinero, of course, with her police connections.

Barney, who was obliged to work with all three women, complained of frost bite.

Police activity in the theatre had quietened down, but had not entirely disappeared. Everyone had been questioned at least once, and a few people twice. Barney had had several sessions with them over whom he saw when Stella was attacked. He made a statement and had signed it; he thought he was believed, but was aware that with the police, as with doctors, you can never be quite sure you are getting the truth.

Barney contented himself with saying: I saw what I saw.

'You see quite a lot of me,' May responded tartly that morning on which Stella was to be, as she had put it herself, 'repatriated'. This was true, for various errands – or he invented them because he liked the place – brought Barney often to the wardrobe room which was on the corridor in which Stella had been attacked.

'He's in love with me,' said Dods placidly. 'Aren't you, Barney?'

'That's right.' Barney and Dods enjoyed a running joke on the subject. Dods was very plain, like a drawing by Cruikshank.

'You're a married man with three children,' accused May, not knowing this was a fable invented by Barney.

'What's that got to do with it?'

'Poor Dods,' said Barney. 'Anyway, this time I have come to feed the cat.'

The theatre cat, thin and bright eyed, who belonged to no one and preferred it that way, lived in a card box on a shelf in the wardrobe room. He was sent out regularly by May to patrol the theatre for mice, came back reporting that there were none, and repaired again to the nice box with a woollen rug. Barney fed him, and Dods brought food from home. 'Out of the mouths of your wife and children,' Barney teased. He knew Dods was not married.

'Haven't you got any girlfriends?' asked May.

'On and off. My career comes first.'

'You are too much under your mother's thumb.'

Barney was indignant. 'No, Alfreda's not like that.'

'Alfreda's just like that. She likes to control everyone and everything.'

'It's a job in this theatre. Anyway, Miss Pinero puts in a very good shout. I don't think anyone bosses Stella.'

'Oh, Stella . . .' May shrugged. 'She's one on her own, isn't she?'

'I don't think you like her.'

'She employs me, pays my wages, and I do the work. Very well, I may say. Liking does not have to come into it.'

'Ouch,' said Dods. 'You're a sharp one.'

May looked as if she would like to say something sharp back, but she bit her lips and turned to her work.

As if asking an innocent question, Barney said: 'Knives are sharp, like the one that went into the two Macs, but can words really be sharp?'

'I know what you are getting at,' said May. 'I barely knew those two.' She looked at them fiercely. 'And if you heard anything else you were wrong.'

Barney and Dods exchanged a glance, both had heard a story about a dog.

'If you mean the story that you swore at them and said you'd get even because they ran over your dog, I did hear that,' said Barney.

'It wasn't my dog.' May made her anger clear. 'It was my mother's, it was old and smelly, and I don't like animals.'

But they did not quite believe her, they knew she did not like dogs, but they knew she loved her mother. But was her mother dead or not?

Silence fell on the room, a quiet little group, each one

thinking about love and the nature of love. It could lead you into dire trouble, that seemed clear to each one.

Alfreda came swinging into the room and once again May found herself envying the long legs which enabled her to wear the short skirt and the long jacket and look good. 'Not working?'

'We are all working,' said Dods, applying himself to the pattern on the table before him. 'Thinking is a vital part of work.'

She ignored this, gave the routine friendly smile at May, which both parties scorned, and spoke to her son. 'Stella's back home, I'm going over there and I want you with me.'

'Should she be working?' asked May, not out of solicitude for Stella, whom she knew would be cosseted, but just to raise an objection, any objection.

'Papers she must sign and letters she will demand to see.'

'Why me?' asked Barney.

'Not because Stella is longing to see you: I want help with carrying my laptop which I might need to use.'

Barney stretched out his arms. 'I'm a good strong boy.' He looked at her with a half smile. 'As you know. Good at carrying, digging and –'

'And talking,' said Alfreda.

'Oh, you've noticed? But I never say the wrong thing.'

May gave a derisive laugh. 'Hark at them, Dods, like a pair of cross-talk comedians.'

'I didn't see any jokes there,' said Dods.

Alfreda said gently: 'Don't take any notice of us, May. I have to bully him a little bit . . . which reminds me, what are you doing in here, Barney?'

'Feeding the cat.' He rustled a bag.

The cat, hearing the noise which it associated with fish, leapt from its box. As it did so, it dislodged another box on the shelf above.

The box, longer than wider, spun in the air, and deposited its contents in a clatter on the floor.

All four, Alfreda, Barney, May and Dods, stared, for the moment silenced. Then Dods spoke.

'Oh Lordy, Lordy.'

Blood is always blood, however dried and brown. Somehow it spreads a sinister penumbra.

Stella came home with a nurse to settle her and see she was comfortable; the nurse would stay all day but go off duty in the evening. Stella was to keep quiet.

'I am here so you could come home, that was the bargain, so don't kick,' said Nurse Sarah Fountain. 'If I had my way you would still be in hospital, but you got *your* way. So you have to keep your part of the bargain and behave.'

'Oh, I will, I will,' said Stella, leaning back against a mountain of pillows and looking appealing. She reached out her hand to pick up the script on which she wanted to work. 'How does my nose look?'

'Good. It's going down nicely.'

'So I can play Cyrano de Bergerac?'

Sarah did not know what Stella meant, so, sensibly, she did not answer. 'You can't play for the moment, remember.'

In spite of his promise to be with her when she came home, Coffin had not turned up but instead had sent a message of apology, he'd be home as soon as he could.

'Where's your good man?' asked Sarah, 'thought he was going to be here?'

Stella was philosophical, she knew what he was up to: he was busying himself in the murder of the Macintoshes and Harry Trent's part in it. If he had a part. 'He's busy,' she said to Sarah. 'He'll be here.' Or, he'll telephone, that was very likely. He was taking part in an investigation that he should have left to the CID department; he was the Chief Commander, no longer a detective, but he couldn't keep away.

She understood, even admired him for it. Nor could she complain that she had married him in ignorance of this side of his character.

'You told me, didn't you?' she addressed him silently. 'Before we married. And I knew anyway. How many years have I known you and you don't change.' Probably it was wives who always said: But I didn't know how it was going to be. 'I didn't know,' Stella continued her silent discussion with the man who was not there. 'I did not know it would hurt.' But then she reflected that she herself had an unpredictable professional life that kept her away, sometimes without warning, so they were equal really. There was a little soothing satisfaction in that.

It seemed only fair.

Had she told him all about everything? Her own guilty conscience gave a throb. She hadn't had a guilty conscience before she got married. It was something you acquired on marriage, she reflected.

'Say something, dear?' asked Nurse Sarah.

'Just cleared my throat.'

'And a perfect throat it is, too.'

God, is she a lesbian? Stella asked herself in a flutter.

'Dr Goldfinch said that you had the most splendid sterno mastoid muscles he had ever seen. He thought it came from projecting your voice on the stage. Do you sing as well?'

'Not often,' said Stella weakly.

'I'm hoping to move over to medicine as a mature student. I hope that doesn't seem crazy to you?' A slight blush appeared on Nurse Sarah's cheek. 'I have started on preliminary work already. Dr Goldfinch has sort of encouraged me . . . we will probably set up practice together.'

Not lesbian, just keen. 'Not a bit. I think it's brave of you.'

'It *is* brave, all the rest of the class will be straight from school.'

'You'll know more than they do,' said Stella, anxious to make amends for her private suspicions. The trouble with her theatre was that you suspected deviant sex everywhere. Nor were you always wrong. Stella remembered one production when she had looked round the assembled cast and said to herself that there wasn't one real man among them. The tradition that the leading lady always slept with her leading man was more honoured in the breach these days than in the observance. She half repressed a giggle.

'Your throat again,' said Nurse Sarah. 'Take a drink of water. Or shall I make you a cup of tea?'

'I think I hear him now . . . you get off, I'm sure you want to be home.'

Sarah Fountain acknowledged that this was so. 'I have

some studying to do and Dr Goldfinch has promised to help with a paper I have to write.'

'Away with you then.'

She watched Sarah Fountain put her coat on, then heard her voice talking to Coffin on the stairs.

'Thank goodness you've come and she's gone.'

'Don't you like her?' He came to sit on the bed beside her. 'She came from a very good agency.'

'Lovely woman and a splendid nurse, but she's costing me a fortune. Private nurses don't come cheap. She's going over to medicine, the doctors' side, that's why she wants to earn the money.' She studied his face. 'Come on, out with it, and stop plucking at the expensive silk on my sheets. Out with it.'

'The weapon has been found . . . And it was in the wardrobe room at the theatre.'

Stella was silent for a moment. That must be why Alfreda had sent a message saying she would be late coming in with production costs she wanted to see. 'Damn. I was hoping it would turn up miles away and have nothing to do with the theatre.'

'It's always looked as if the murderer knew the theatre.' Coffin was sympathetic. 'And this pinpoints it. Who goes in the wardrobe and design room?'

'Oh, everyone, so many people need to go in there to see the clothes, try them on if they are performing in them, the dressers, the designers. Anyone, really.'

'It's not kept locked?'

'It's supposed to be kept locked when empty, for security reasons . . . we have had losses . . . but I doubt if that is kept to rigidly. Alfreda would know.'

'So, really, there would be no trouble, or not much, about salting away the weapon after the crime?'

'No. What is it? You haven't said.'

'It came from one of the props used in *Oh What a Lovely War* . . . a bayonet.'

'I thought they were plastic,' said Stella in a weak voice.

'Not all; apparently the producer insisted that one or two performers carry the real thing.'

175

'They should have been blunted.'

'They were, but this one was sharpened up again. It shows on the blade.'

Stella shivered. 'How horribly premeditated. But at least you have the weapon.'

'Yes.' Coffin stood up. 'I don't think Lewinder is best pleased with his team for not finding it earlier . . . still, he's hopeful of some forensic help from it. It does happen. Not nearly as often as I could wish.'

They looked at each other, and both knew that he was thinking of Harry Trent who might or might not have been in the theatre corridor which led to the wardrobe rooms on the night Stella had been attacked. He could have been the one to take the bayonet from wherever it had been hidden among the robes, meaning, no doubt, to take it right away, but obliged because of the commotion around Stella to hide it elsewhere. Anywhere, the first place that offered.

'Of course, I shall have to leave it all to Lewinder,' Coffin said, regretfully. 'We shall consult, naturally.' That was more like it, Stella thought. 'He will keep me informed.'

'What about Harry?'

'I haven't seen him, we need a rest from each other. Too many unanswered and some unasked questions between us at the moment. But one of his Greenwich colleagues called on him. George Ferguson sent a sergeant who has worked with Harry. George is a good sort, he'll handle it well. It seems Harry was sitting in the kitchen, not saying much. He's been told to stay where he is.'

'Will he do that?'

'They are keeping an eye on him,' said Coffin. 'He's being watched.'

Stella was thoughtful: 'He'll be all right, won't he?'

Coffin knew exactly what she meant. 'He won't kill himself. The report said he was content.' The word had in fact been 'happy', but John Coffin found that word unacceptable. The Harry he had travelled that long day with could not have been happy. Exhausted, accepting, maybe, but not happy.

Ruefully, he reflected that whenever he touched Harry there was a contradiction, rising up to hit him. Inside him,

176

he admitted to deeper feeling: Why should Harry be happy, when I am not.

Then Stella, smiling at him and holding his hand, reminded him that he had one reason to be happy. A reason for happiness, a reason for anxiety: he had got his secretary to postpone his appointment with his doctor. Dr Keith Foster was no doubt at that moment calling him a coward, but he would have to wait.

Stella said: 'Why don't you telephone Max and order a meal . . . he can send it over. You won't want to cook and I am supposed to be resting.'

'Good idea.' He stood up.

'And I think Alfreda may be bringing in some financial matters for me to look at.'

'That is not such a good idea. And she may be late, Lewinder will be talking to her.'

'I know, I worked that one out for myself, but she will come. She might have supper with us. Order extra food.'

'All right, I'll go down to the kitchen, check what we need . . . I did some shopping . . . or Ellen did; she made a casserole but that will keep, and then I will call Max. What would you like to eat?'

Stella was vague. 'Anything delicious, darling. You choose, make it a surprise . . . I'm not supposed to drink, by the way, but I don't think a mouthful of champagne would count, do you?'

Laughing, Coffin went downstairs to the kitchen. The kitchen was two flights down the tower in which they lived. The front door was one flight further down still; it was an inconvenient way of living, but it had charm and you certainly kept slim, Coffin thought. He had his hand on the wall telephone when it rang, he hesitated, would it be Lewinder, or even Harry Trent, then he answered it.

An angry voice spoke loudly. 'You are a coward.'

Dr Keith Foster knew how to be sharp.

'I know.' Coffin was prepared to be humble when it suited him. 'But there is something else on my mind at the moment. I have made another appointment. That will be kept.' Then he said: 'Haven't you *any* idea about the results yet? Can't you say something?' Anything, he thought, that gave a clue. Wouldn't it be good to be offered relief. But no, Foster was firm.

'I want to see you, we have to speak.'

Damn, Coffin thought, the results are bad then. He kept silent for a moment.

'I ought to cross you off my list as a difficult patient.'

'You won't though.'

'No.' And suddenly Keith lightened the whole mood, he laughed. 'Not if you promise to fill me in on the affair of the anonymous man . . . My spies tell me an arrest is imminent.'

'You are ahead of me then,' said Coffin, but he felt better. Perhaps he wasn't due to die just yet. All the same, what was this about an arrest? A call to Superintendent Phil Lewinder seemed indicated, but Max and Stella's supper came first.

He rang Max in a better mood, and obliged Stella by asking for a bottle of champagne to go with the salmon and the salad. A light meal, surely she ought not to eat too much?

He had hardly finished speaking when the doorbell rang, a long commanding peal.

Coffin ran down the stairs to let in Alfreda and Barney. 'Come in, Stella is expecting you.'

'Sorry we are late . . . You will know why.' She looked white, but Barney looked flushed and excited.

Coffin nodded. 'I know. You were there?'

'In the room when the cat knocked the box over. If it hadn't been for the cat, I suppose no one would have looked in that box.'

Perhaps it should have been searched before, Coffin thought, we were looking everywhere, so I will want to know why not. As will Phil Lewinder. 'Go on up, Stella is in bed. You know the way?'

'I will carry up your laptop, then go,' volunteered Barney.

'Stella wondered if you would like to stay and eat with us?'

'No, but thank you.' Alfreda smiled, she was pleased to be asked. 'I need to get back on the job.'

'I will bring some drinks up, then.' Coffin looked at Barney. 'Stay and have one.'

Barney bounced up the stairs behind his mother. 'We're in, we're in,' he half sang under his breath. It was the nearest to a friendship with Stella Pinero that he, and his mother too, had got.

'Shut up,' ordered Alfreda. 'They will hear you.'

He drew level with her on the stairs, almost pushing her against the wall. 'Were you upset at the way the bayonet turned up?'

'Yes. I thought you were too.'

He considered. 'I was and I wasn't. A bit of me was alarmed, but another side was excited. Funny, isn't it?'

'Not to me.' Alfreda moved past him and knocked on the door of Stella's room.

Stella was leaning against her pillows, examining her face in a large hand mirror. Her nose was still troubling her, but a good foundation cream would cover a lot. But she would photograph badly for some time unless carefully lit. She considered her engagements for the next few weeks. A voice-over and a radio play, but nothing that would show up a badly swollen nose.

She welcomed Alfreda, nodded at Barney, and seized her letters. Alfreda sat down with her laptop on a chair beside her, ready to take dictation if necessary. Barney stared around the room. He liked the pale ivory and sepia of the silks on the bed and at the windows, giving them ten marks for subtlety; he thought the furniture too plain, but it looked good and possibly it was better style than being too frilly and fussy. He knew he had a lot to learn in matters of taste. Alfreda had none in his opinion.

Stella looked at her letters while questioning Alfreda about the discovery of the weapon.

'It was nasty,' Alfreda admitted. 'Brought everything very close. I felt sick and May nearly fainted. You know she's such a tough one as a rule. I think she thought she was going to be arrested on the spot . . . Well, she is the one who has easiest access to those boxes. There's Dods, of course, but he's been away sick and only just back.'

'I wondered about that sickness,' said Stella.

'Because of a new man in his life? No, I think it was genuine, he has had a terrible cough and I saw he had prescription pills to take. No, I wouldn't suspect Dods.'

'I wouldn't suspect May,' said Stella. 'I mean, what possible motive could she have?'

'There was the death of the dog,' said Alfreda thoughtfully.

A voice from the window said: 'She's lived in Spinnergate all her life, she said so. If a person has lived here that long, and so had the Macs, both sorts, first dead, second dead, there might be a motive no one knew about. Or there might be no motive at all, just an enjoyment of killing. Maybe she's a twin or something and needed to kill two people who matched.'

'That's a disgusting idea,' said Stella, very disturbed by what she heard.

Alfreda did not answer.

Downstairs, Coffin was about to bring up a tray with drinks on it, when the telephone rang once more.

'Coffin here.'

'Superintendent Lewinder would like to speak to you,' said his secretary. 'He's in the office.'

'Put him on. Yes? What is it?'

'I wanted to tell you this myself, sir. We have detained a man pushing a blue bike who claims to be Mark Trent. Yes, sir, he walked into Fleming Street Substation, and he came in pushing a blue bike.'

14

It would be idle to pretend that Hyde did not know now that the end was near. He could feel it because Hyde was getting beyond control, popping out when it was least desirable. It had been painful as they had come so close to each other, but Hyde saw now that Jekyll was going to be eaten up.

Perhaps it had always been obvious from the beginning that one of them would consume the other. Obvious to Hyde, but not to Jekyll who, at that stage, did not know that Hyde existed. A curtain came down over Hyde after the big bang that had given him birth. Hyde remembered enough of this even to know he had been created by it. 'I was a child,' Hyde said, 'and I became a monster.'

Jekyll did not know Hyde although Hyde knew the presence of Jekyll. Hyde was in retirement for years after the first arrival on the scene; this made things easier for the pair.

It was only on his re-emergence, revival if you like, that Hyde realized he had a function, that he was there to do a job. But that moment of awareness was the crack through which Jekyll crept. As any animal knows, self-consciousness is double edged; you can know too much about yourself. What Hyde knew, so Jekyll began to know. Little disquieting touches of knowledge, almost as if they had come from an alien world. Anger, which turned to violence, and was enjoyed. A memory of hate. But also the satisfactory feeling that what had been done was right to have been done.

Mix that self-justification in together with guilt and the

mixture is dangerous for Jekyll, for Hyde and for any who comes between the two.

'Hail horrors, hail,' the poet said. 'The mind is its own place and in itself, can make a heaven of hell, a hell of heaven.'

15

What John Coffin would have liked to do was to go back up the stairs, get rid of Alfreda and Barney, then settle down to a quiet drink with Stella. Not champagne, it was not one of his favoured drinks, although he recognized that to Stella it meant celebration and joy.

What he had to do was to move out the Boxers, mother and son, wait for Max to deliver the food, eat as much as he could in a short time, then settle Stella with books and music and the television set while he went to see the man who called himself Mark Trent.

As he walked up the stairs, he found himself wondering what his mother would make of him and his career if she had still been alive. Of course, she could still be alive for all he knew, although he hardly dared to think what age she would be. He came of a long-lived family, he was sure of that, but of little else in his family.

Oh, and the cat and dog, they had to be attended to somehow. Well, the dog could come, unless he opted to sit on the bed with Stella where he would certainly be joined by the cat.

He was passed on the stairs by the cat on the way down, behind whom were Alfreda and Barney.

'Barney felt a bit offish, shock, I suppose, so I'm taking him home.'

Coffin stood back so they could pass. 'Oh, I'm sorry. Anything I can do?'

'No, I'll just get him home.' Alfreda smiled nervously. 'I didn't tire Miss Pinero out, I was careful. I left her with a few figures to think about.'

He saw them down the stairs and then went up the staircase to Stella again. 'They're off. Did you send them away?' He began to open the champagne.

'No, Alfreda went through all that was necessary with me, attendances up, there didn't seem any trouble, one or two questions about finance and casting. Equity is being a difficulty as usual, although of course I see their point, and then Alfreda stood up and off they went. She was thinking about me, I expect.'

The champagne popped open. 'I did tell her to give you an easy run.'

Stella studied his face. 'Those telephone calls that you took downstairs . . . It's the case, isn't it? I can tell from your expression. Don't let it gnaw at you.'

Something is, Coffin thought, but maybe it has surgical teeth in it.

'I wish you would retire,' said Stella, sipping her champagne.

'I will if you will.'

'Oh, performers never retire, they go on and on, until one day they pack their bags and disappear. And after a while someone says: Haven't seen old Dolly lately, or old Micky.'

'I suppose old detectives are the same.' He himself might be retired by life quite soon. You took health for granted until a question arose, and you had to face what might be a blunt truth. 'After we have eaten . . . salmon and salad, by the way, I have to go out.'

Stella finished her champagne. 'You go now. The salmon will keep, I'm not hungry yet. We will eat when you come back. You will come back? With you, I never know.'

One day, she thought, he will go out and not come back. And that could be the truth.

When Coffin walked into the room, the man was standing looking out of the window, his back to the room. He was tall, about the same height as Coffin, which made him slightly taller than Harry, but when he swung round there was the face. The same face. Except that it was leaner, and unshaved, it was Harry's face. Hair was longer, hands dirtier.

184

Manner wilder, but, and Coffin found he had to say this, marginally saner than Harry had looked these last days.

Coffin began to introduce himself but the man interrupted him. 'I know who you are, I was told you were coming. Harry talked about you . . . in the days when we talked, which hasn't been easy lately. I tried to talk the other day, hung around till I could get at him, but he acted as though I had the plague.' A wicked smile flicked across Mark's face. 'Mind you, I did act it up a bit, gave him the works, I wanted to put the wind up him, give him a scare. I've never really liked the law enforcer.'

'I know your brother. And I am very pleased to know you.' To know you really exist; I had wondered.

'It isn't true that if you know him, you know me. We ain't alike.'

'I have noticed,' said Coffin politely. But more alike than you might think. 'Do sit down. He was looking for you.'

'So I heard, word got around.' Mark sat down opposite Coffin and lit a cigarette. He was wearing torn jeans and thick grey sweater; there was a certain style there, though. By no means as casual as you would have me think, decided Coffin. Offered a cigarette, he refused. 'No, thank you.'

'I went across the river to see him; he wasn't there, the house all shut up, looked empty. So I left my bike there, and went for a walk. When I came back, I'll swear he was there, or had been.' He shook his head. 'No answer, though.'

'You know about the murders? The Macintoshes, the real ones and pseudo ones?'

'Is that what you call them, the pseudo ones? Nice classy name for them. 'Course, I know, everyone does. What do you think I went to see Harry for? We lived with the old ones once.' A little of the bounce had left Merry, and his face was troubled.

Coffin nodded. 'Harry told me.'

'He's been in an odd state, has Harry. Although he wouldn't like to know this, his wife got hold of me and asked me to see him if I could, she said he was in a funny state. He was on sick leave.'

Coffin gave him a long look.

'Yes, all right, I get what you think: I still played him up, but he gets under my skin. He had me down for a murder in Woolwich; don't ask me why I got elected for that honour.'

'You two really don't like each other very much, do you?'

Mark shrugged. 'It's not easy being a twin. I like him better than he likes me. Trust now, that's another matter.' He took a long puff at his cigarette. 'Do you know what got me in here? I heard the police were after a man with a blue bike, after him for abusing a child. I wasn't best pleased, and I saw Harry behind that.'

'Not altogether,' said Coffin. 'Who told you the story?'

'The old biddy that sells newspapers by the underground station. She saw me riding past.'

'Mimsie Marker,' said Coffin. Who else?

'Seeing it was her that I hired the bike from, she had an interest in telling me, I suppose. So I turned myself in. Always better to get in first. Mind you, I felt a strong blue arm hovering over my collar as I came through the street,' he added sardonically. 'Although in my experience it's easier to get into these places than to get out.'

'Where are you staying?'

'I have a room in an old dosshouse, Harry knows where, I told him. And I'm working; Jim Foster took me on as driver in his haulage firm. I know him of old, we went to school round here for a while, the pair of us, and Jim was a friend. I like this district, it suits me, I like the sort of life I can have here. I don't want to settle, so I come back when I feel like tasting the flavour of it again.'

He had a way with words, Coffin thought. 'And Harry doesn't come back?'

For the first time, Merry did not meet his eyes, he looked out of the window. 'Dunno about that, couldn't say. Maybe he does.'

Brother suspects brother in this case, Coffin thought, and who's to say which is right?

'May I see your wrists?'

Merry looked at Coffin, then pulled up his sleeves and extended both hands.

The scar was there, on the left wrist. Right, it had been on Harry. Right twin, left twin.

'You left-handed?'

'Yes.'

A similar scar, but different.

Coffin nodded towards the red mark. 'How did you get that?'

'Did it myself.' He pulled the sleeve down, hiding his wrist. 'Got what you want?'

'More or less.'

'Right, I think I'll have another shot at seeing Harry,' said Merry, standing up.

'No, I shouldn't do that, leave it a while. And I'd like to talk to you later, so . . .'

He looked at Merry Trent, and Merry nodded. 'I know,' he sighed. 'Like I said: easier to get into here than to get out.'

Phil Lewinder stood up for the Chief Commander. The boss looks bad, he thought. Exhausted. He's taking this murder too much to heart. Shrewdly, he added: It all goes back to the theatre his wife runs, he knows it, and that is what worries him.

Lewinder was half right.

He had to admit that in a wry kind of way, he himself was enjoying it, or at least, he was finding it exceedingly interesting. It was a real puzzler.

'What did you make of him, sir?' Although Lewinder had not been privy to the darker imaginings of John Coffin about Harry and his twin, he knew enough to know there were problems. 'A bit different from his brother. Not in looks, two for a pair, there, but way of life.'

'They may not be so very different underneath,' said Coffin. 'I want to talk to him again, but I suggest he goes back to where he is staying and I see him tomorrow. Get Harry Trent in too if he is up to it. Has a doctor seen him?'

'I believe so, and taken him off some of the medication that was playing banjos in his mind.'

Coffin nodded. 'Bloody drugs.' But it wasn't all drugs

waltzing around in Harry's mind and he knew it, even if Lewinder did not. Although meeting Lewinder's calm, sceptical eyes, he wondered. Hard to fool, Lewinder.

'I don't think we could hold the brother, there seems absolutely nothing to charge him with. The child molesting charge will not stand up, the girl accuser is a known liar who has tried it before. We ought to have her in here if anyone,' said Lewinder vengefully. She had given him trouble before, even accusing one of his own officers. 'She's not stupid either, she goes to one of the best schools in the borough; my own girl goes to it.' He slapped his hand on a magazine with a composite photograph of children's faces on the front. 'My girl edited this, jubilee edition, to celebrate fifty years.'

'What I want to do is to see the two brothers together.'

'No firm evidence, no evidence we could use that either of them killed the Macintoshes. Yet there they both are, wired up in the case.' Lewinder was not usually given to poetic imagery. 'I don't know Harry Trent, although I had heard of him as a good officer. I don't know what to think. Meanwhile, all the routine investigation is going on: might be of interest that a fingerprint has been brought up on the card found with the dead pair in the theatre . . .'

'Any matches with anything, anyone?'

'Hope to try it on the bayonet . . . Of course, if the rest of the gun, from which the bayonet was taken, could be found, that would be a help. Probably long since burnt, but teams are searching dustbins and the local rubbish dump. Not hopeful, though. Anyway,' he added gloomily, 'only a fool would not use gloves.'

'Must have taken some force extracting the actual bayonet from the stock of the gun.' Would the theatre face a claim for compensation from the museum for the destruction of what might be a valuable exhibit? Stella would not be pleased.

'Not really, judging by the other of the pair that were on loan from the local museum . . . nearly a hundred years old and the wood was rotten. Shows planning, though, not a spontaneous let's-get-them-now-mood kind of killing.'

'I never thought that for a minute,' said Coffin, who saw a darker and deeper picture.

He found himself staring thoughtfully at the school magazine with the crowd of young faces looking back at him. 'Can I borrow the magazine? I'll take care of it.'

Lewinder handed it over proudly. 'Have it, sir, keep it. My girl Merinda will be pleased. I've got several copies.'

Of course you have, Coffin thought, the parent–child relationship could be very strong. Stronger than the sibling bond? Stronger than the twin relationship?

Stella was asleep when he got home, but she woke up when he came into the room. 'I'm hungry,' she declared.

'So am I. I'll bring up a tray.' He tossed the school magazine on the bed. 'Have a look at that, look at the faces on the cover and see if it gives you any ideas.'

He returned smartly with a tray from which savoury, fishy smells floated. 'I put it all, vegetables as well, into the microwave as you taught me.'

'Smells delicious.' Stella settled herself on her pillows. 'Talk first, or eat first?'

'I can do both,' answered Coffin, aware that he was exceedingly hungry.

'I wondered at first what you wanted me to see, and then I thought it must be the faces.'

'I knew I had married an intelligent woman,' said Coffin through a mouthful of hot salmon, it was a little too hot so that he gave a small gasp as well.

'You've trained me.' Stella pointed to a young girl's face. 'Is that or is it not Alfreda aged about eleven?'

Coffin nodded, he was pleased. 'I thought so.' He let his eyes search the page again. Oh yes, he saw what he thought he saw. 'And would you say that those were the twins, aged not so much older?'

Stella leaned forward to study the picture. 'Can't be sure. Could be any boys.' She considered. 'But they do look very alike, but boys that age . . .'

Coffin was also thoughtful. One last hurdle to cross, he decided. He wished he didn't feel so tired.

189

'Children who experience violence can become violent adults, so I'm told,' he said. The thought served to take the taste out of the salmon with tarragon sauce. Stella looked at him with affection, then she said gently that she was very tired now, perhaps they could talk more in the morning.

She let him rearrange the pillows and adjust the light. Poor love, she thought, as he walked away with the tray. He is really up against it. I wish he didn't mind things so much. It's just a job, isn't it, after all? But she knew for him it was not and never had been just a job.

Coffin was in the kitchen, pushing the dirty plates into the dishwasher, watched by the cat who hoped for some salmon scraps, when the telephone rang.

It was Lewinder. 'Sorry to disturb you so late, but one of my keen young men just called me.' Coffin looked at the kitchen clock. Yes, very keen. 'There is a print on the bayonet. Blurred, but he thinks it is a match for the one on the card. Probably a thumbprint and there might be a scar on it.'

16

It was raining in the morning, the thick heavy rain that brought mist with it. Down at Spinnergate underground station, Mimsie Marker huddled under her big umbrella and even considered retiring. But she knew she would not, death would have to do the job for her. Since that seemed likely if she caught pneumonia, she took a draught of hot tea, laced with whisky, from her big Thermos flask which she always kept by her side.

Alfreda Boxer and Barney walked round to the theatre together, they did not keep a car, and both were done up in heavy raincoats. They had stayed up late talking, then neither of them had slept well. 'I'm thinking of moving out, Ma,' said Barney, 'taking my own place. Get a room somewhere.'

'Can you afford it?' She knew only too well that Stella did not pay him much, and that he was usually in debt.

'No, won't stop me, though.'

'If it's what you want.' Alfreda put her head down and galloped through the rain.

'Be best.'

Alfreda said: 'I'll get things going, then I will come back and help you pack.'

'Ta. Be grateful.'

They hurried on to the theatre. On the way, they were joined by May Renier who had no umbrella and no raincoat, and said she did not mind getting wet.

'You look too miserable for words, May,' said Alfreda.

'Feel it. The past catches up with you sometimes, doesn't it?'

'Certainly does, the thing is to run fast.'

191

'If you can.'

'Shut up, May, you're making me as gloomy as yourself.' Alfreda studied May's face. 'You do look rotten.'

'I was sick in the night. Takes me like that sometimes.'

'Don't stay long, just do what is necessary and then get home.'

'I think I will do. Thanks. It was the news, you see. I couldn't take it somehow.'

Alfreda managed a smile as they walked into the theatre. They passed Dods deep in conversation with the doorman. It was the doorman who had picked up the news about the fingerprint from a young constable to whom he was remotely related and who had heard the news from his girlfriend who was a secretary in the police offices. The doorman had passed on his news with speed to all he could reach, so that a furious Lewinder later complained that almost all the theatre had known before he had.

Nothing in life goes exactly as you think it will, so that John Coffin was obliged to step back for a while from the interference he was conducting into the case that Lewinder was managing. A major financial muddle in the main accounting department took him several hours that morning when he had planned to interview several people. The word fraud was being freely bandied around, so that he must take notice while gritting his teeth.

So it was almost midday by the time he saw Mark Trent.

'Sorry to keep you waiting,' he said as he went into the bleak interview room.

Mark shrugged. 'Doesn't matter. I've already lost a day's wages; I might as well sit around here as anywhere else in Spinnergate.'

Coffin frowned. 'Where's your brother? I want to talk to you both, and together.'

Merry was interested but not anxious. 'I don't know about you, but I've been telephoning him all morning and couldn't get him.'

The woman detective sergeant with Coffin (carefully selected for her tact and good looks by Lewinder as Coffin's aide

192

that morning) murmured: 'Inspector Trent was told last night you wanted to see him this morning and he agreed; the superintendent sent a car up to collect him, but the house was empty.'

Even as she spoke, the door opened and Harry Trent came in. He looked refreshed and cheerful, a different man from the one Coffin had last seen falling into exhausted sleep.

'Am I late? Since the doc took me off that drug that was buggering me up, I've felt fine. An allergic reaction, he called it, but I think I was poisoned . . . So I went for an early morning walk in the park at Greenwich and across the heath; I went too far. But I am here now.'

Not only fit and full of energy, Coffin thought, feeling none of these things himself, but there was something else . . . he was happy as well. It seemed unfair.

'Sit down, please,' he said, taking control of the interview. He introduced the woman detective and explained that the interview would be taped: 'I want to talk to you first, Mark.' Harry started to say something. 'Be quiet and just listen, Harry, you did your talking the other day.'

He turned to Mark, whom he would always think of as Merry. 'I have seen a photograph of you two as boys at school here, close by the girl's face, about the same age. I think you knew that girl.' He held up a hand. 'All right, don't say anything yet, either of you, but when you do I want the truth.'

There was a moment's pause. Then he said: 'I always had the feeling that there was a hidden agenda with you two. All right, Harry was looking for you, Merry, and he had some drug-induced stories. I am not saying he did not believe them, they were fantasy world, but the violence they were rooted in was real enough, and it went back to your childhood here. So he was looking for you, and you, Merry, were looking for what?'

Merry sat silent. 'Both of you knew more about the other one's movements and motives than you've said, of that I am convinced. So, Merry, back to where it begins, and tell it as it was.'

'The beginning?'

'The very beginning is your childhood here, but I want to know about the death of the elder Macintoshes, the real ones. Tell me what you know.'

'I don't see why I should talk.'

'I think so,' said Coffin gently. 'You could go to prison for murder, their murder . . . we have a fingerprint.'

'Not mine,' said Merry quickly; he did not look at Harry, but his brother was staring at him.

'We shall have to see about that. Remember you are in a position of inferiority here, you have business to discuss.'

'All right, I saw them when they were dead. They were both in the house where we had lived. I went back, I often went back, not to see them, just because that house was built into my brain . . .'

'You knew the daughter, why not say so?'

'All right, I knew her. I'm not saying any more. I'd kept in touch with her . . . there was a reason for that.'

Coffin nodded. 'All right, go on.'

'I went back . . . I looked through a window and saw them lying around in the living room. He was slumped across the table, she was on the floor. They had been there for some time . . .'

'Go on.'

'I got into the house, there were always ways.'

'No one saw you?'

'You've got to remember that all the area round there had been cleared, the house was an island, all the old neighbours gone. I don't know how long they had been dead, some time, I think. I could see that there had been blows to the face and the head. There had been a fight, I thought.'

'So what did you do?'

'Nothing. I left them there.'

'You didn't tell the police, didn't think it your duty to report what you had seen?'

Merry was silent. 'I thought it was Harry who had killed them . . . We didn't see each other much, but I always felt I knew what was going on in his mind, because I felt the same. We were both angry. I always knew he was capable of violence.'

194

'Why?'

'He went into the police.'

'Not a good reason,' said Coffin.

'No? But it would have balanced some violence inside him. Kept him straight . . . He had always hated the Macs, but in a way he loved them too.'

Coffin had his eye on Harry Trent who was listening intently. What was Harry making of all this?

'I know I seem disturbed by all that went on when we were kids, they could be cold, those Macs, but my madness is eccentricity . . . on the surface. It goes deeper with Harry.'

'It doesn't end there, though, does it?'

'I walked the streets, wondering what to do. Then I went back to bury them . . . Alfreda was there, she trusted me and she didn't trust many. Bad feelings in that house, bad, bad feelings. Good people, and they were good in a way, can be wicked and dangerous too. She said there had been a quarrel, she had hit them and they had hit her. She had left them alive, but had come back to find them slumped about the room. Dead. Where's the boy, I said. She always had the boy around. She said she'd sent him off. But he'd been there all right.'

Lovely, thought Coffin, what a scenario. Two dead bodies, Alfreda, probably high on something, and Merry. Also one adolescent.

'So I helped her bury them. In the garden. It wasn't until we had done the job that we found the note, which I did not handle. Seemed to say, that after all, they had killed themselves.'

'Did you believe it?'

Merry was silent. Then he said: 'I wanted to.'

'A more recent fingerprint has been brought up on it,' said Coffin, thoughtfully. 'Remember it was found at the scene of the other murder of the other Macs. This is a two-layer investigation, don't forget.'

'I don't know anything about that, but on that other occasion, I felt the presence of someone else there. Harry, I thought. I didn't know what to make of Alfreda's story, I didn't believe it, I thought Harry had done it.'

There's always layers and layers in the truth, thought Coffin, you have to peel it away like an onion. And like an onion you can smell it; I can smell the truth now. Also like an onion, it makes you want to cry.

Harry suddenly stood up. 'Speak for yourself, you're a liar!' He lunged forward and hit Merry in the face. Once and then again, hard blows. Merry staggered back with blood pouring down his face.

Coffin got between them, pushing Harry back. 'Are you hurt?' he asked Merry.

'I'm bleeding, aren't I?'

Harry went to his brother, put his arm round his shoulders, and began to dab his nose with a handkerchief. 'Sorry, bro.'

'I'm sorry too.'

The blood was on both of them and blood, as Coffin reflected, was thicker than water.

'Did you kill them?' Coffin asked Harry. 'The truth, please.'

'No.'

'But you knew they were dead?'

Harry thought about his answer. 'Guessed it,' he said.

Underneath the surface anger and show of violence, there was a confidence in Harry Trent that Coffin had not seen earlier. And a touch of happiness.

He did not know what to make of that, perhaps being back with his twin again, the two sides reunited.

One layer of the mystery was unfolding, but bringing puzzles with it.

'That hidden agenda,' he said. 'What brought you both back here? What was it you both knew that made you think the dead were not really buried.'

'I was sick,' said Harry.

'Yes, I accept that. But Merry was here too, and he wasn't sick; he says he likes the district, likes to come back. I accept that too. But look at what actually happened, not what you both say.' He stopped to give weight to his words. 'Two people, who had adopted the same name and who lived in the same house as the earlier dead pair, were killed. That is what happened.'

They remained silent, Merry held the handkerchief to his

196

nose, but he was relaxed, his brother's arm around his shoulders.

Coffin studied them, then drew the interview to an end. Won't get much more out of Tweedledum and Tweedledee just now, he thought.

'I must ask you to stay here. I expect Superintendent Lewinder will want to talk to you. I will see some coffee comes in. Unless you would rather have tea?'

Then he said: 'Would you mind letting me see your hands, please? No, not the wrists, I saw those scars before. Palms upmost, please.'

Each twin held their hands so that Coffin could see them. On neither thumb, left hand, right hand, left-handed twin, right-handed twin, was there a scar.

Coffin sighed. 'I shall have to see the woman,' he decided. But he had known that anyway. Better get on with this case, he told himself, get it finished. Or I shall be too busy to die.

May Renier took herself home, she still felt sick, she recognized the signs of a full-blown migraine developing. Emotion did that to you.

She had not liked Joe and Josie, and one of them had killed her mother's dog, but she found herself missing them. If they had been there, outside the theatre, with their stall, she would have bought a hot cup of coffee. Or even an ice-cream. Oddly enough, a frozen lolly had been known to combat nausea and limit the headache.

Which goes to show it's emotion, she said to herself. I am too highly strung.

She walked home, it was still raining, and called out to her mother as she went in: 'Hello, Mum, here I am!'

Her mother did not answer. No answer was expected, indeed, it might have alarmed May if a spectral voice had called back to her, but her own greeting made May feel at home.

Home was important, it was where you were most yourself.

She lay on her bed, thinking how glad she was that she had been brave enough to send a message to Superintendent

Lewinder that she was ill and could not be interviewed today.

She had to decide first what to say and what not to say. No wonder she felt ill, like two people, really. One of whom could be cured by an ice-cream lolly and the other of whom would ache for ever.

Alfreda had been kind. She must remember that kindness, and not probe into it too deeply. Sometimes the surface was best.

Phil Lewinder was embarrassed to have to report to the Chief Commander that May Renier was too ill to talk to anyone and that Alfreda Boxer was not in her office.

Theatre people were very hard to lay your hands on, he decided, they seemed to have a knack of never being where they should be when you wanted them.

He sent a car with a woman detective in it to where Alfreda Boxer lived.

'Bring her in with you,' he said.

'Certainly, sir.' She was a gentle but efficient girl, tougher than she appeared.

Alfreda and Barney had a well-protected front door, needed no doubt in this part of London. You walked straight into the hall and talked through an entry phone to announce your arrival.

In the hall was a trunk, neatly bound up, with a suitcase by its side.

She tried the phone, pressed the button and named herself. Dead silence. Of course, sometimes such phones did not work, but to her surprise the door was unlocked, so she marched in to bang on an inner door. No answer. Silence.

A head poked out the door on the other side of the landing. 'Shouldn't bother, dear, they've gone.' The head belonged to a lady who seemed just to have woken up. 'I lodge here when I'm in a show and can't get the last train back. Alfreda's so jolly about it.'

'When did they go?'

'Oh, just now, dear. You've only just missed them. Luggage left downstairs to be collected. Walking to the tube, I believe, not the day for it, though.'

The news, relayed to Coffin by Lewinder, was received bleakly. 'Send a car to the tube station, and if she is still there, keep her there, I am going down myself.'

Caught and held where she was, she would have no time to think. And with luck, be nervous.

He was there himself within minutes; a police car which had got there before him, was parked at the kerb just by Mimsie Marker who was taking some interest in it.

Coffin went down the escalator which led to a narrow winding passageway to the platform. In the waiting room, were two uniformed police constables and Alfreda Boxer. She was sitting on the bench, her raincoat buttoned to the neck, and wearing dark spectacles. The spectacles in no way disguised her but perhaps were not meant to, but just to hide the expression in her eyes.

She stood up when John Coffin came in. 'Sit down again, please, Alfreda. I need to talk to you.'

He looked round the waiting room, which was brightly and freshly painted and quite warm. Not bad as these things went.

'I expect you are surprised that I want to talk to you instead of Superintendent Lewinder, but I thought as we know each other you might find it easier to talk.' And that's a lie, he admitted to himself, it's that you think you will get more out of her than Lewinder. And underneath that honest appreciation of his motives was one yet more honest: he wanted to be the one that asked the questions and got the answers. God, he felt tired, though.

Alfreda licked her lips but said nothing.

'Are you running away?'

After a while, she said: 'Yes.'

'From whom?'

For the first time, she looked amused. 'You know.'

'All right, you are running away from me. Why?'

He noticed that her gaze wandered round the room as if looking for someone else. He did not have her full attention.

He waited for her to answer. 'Come on.'

She sighed. 'I wasn't looking forward to being arrested. I thought I'd make a run for it, have a good time, eat, drink, see some shows, buy some clothes, take a lover if I can find one in the time . . . I knew you would catch me, but –' and she shrugged – 'I would have something to remember.'

'You admit you tried to kill your parents?'

'You seem to know all about it.'

'I have put a picture together.' The picture had holes in it, as if seen by someone with injured vision, but it was workable. 'You had a quarrel, and attacked them.'

'Yes, that's about it.' She sounded sad. 'They were so rigid, bound into a moral code that had no heart. When I told them I was pregnant, they turned me out. Hard to believe. They gave me money, I wasn't turned out on the street, but I was unpersoned – that's what they used to call it in the old USSR, didn't they? So I became another person, a new name, Boxer.'

'But you went back?'

'Every so often, it was my house after all, left me by my grandfather. But I never forgave them and every time I saw them I got angry.' She shrugged. 'One day I went too far, hit them both with a heavy vase, broke it to bits. I thought I had killed them and ran away . . .'

'But you went back?'

'I went back the same day, more than once. I kept looking, hoping the scene would go away. I didn't tell Merry that. Nor Harry. You keep out of this, I told him. But I didn't know what to do. So I left them. I suppose there was a subtext to that: I liked seeing them lying there. At my mercy. Which I didn't have.'

She looked at him. 'You've got to believe this. They had moved since I first left them unconscious, so I thought they had come round and then died . . . still all my fault.'

'Merry helped you bury them?

'And then you found the suicide note?'

'Yes, where my father had been lying, it was his writing.'

'Didn't it puzzle you?'

'Yes, but I think, just from something he said, that my father may have had cancer. It would be a way out, once they knew I would never come to help them. They were on their own.' Her tone was bleak. She meant it, she had nour-

200

ished a healthy plant of hate and it would go on growing.

'Why did you not then tell the police what had happened?'

'Merry said we couldn't dig them up and to leave it the way it was.'

Of course, because he thought Harry had killed them and never mind the note.

'He was always sweet for me . . . he thought he was Barney's father. Afraid he wasn't. Not quite sure who claims that honour.'

She was still looking round the room as if someone might pop out of a hole somewhere.

'But there are two more deaths to consider.'

Alfreda lowered her eyes. 'Yes. Joe and Josie. I brought them to Spinnergate. Lent them the house. They had trouble of their own and wanted to hide. So I said: "Call yourself by this name and you can have the place for free."'

'So?'

'They started to worry about where my parents were. Word about their worry was picked up by Harry Trent in Greenwich, he had a kind of informer here. He told his brother.'

So that was the hidden agenda, Coffin thought, both brothers knew about the buried bodies. Even when twins disliked each other, they communicated. So they had circled around, observing and wondering what was happening. While Harry had a mini-nervous breakdown.

'So you killed Joe and Josie?'

Alfreda bowed her head.

'I see.' He drew back. 'The constable outside will drive you to see Superintendent Lewinder; he will have questions to ask you.'

He walked towards the door to speak to the uniformed constable outside on the platform. A train had just come and gone.

'Where is Barney?'

She shook her head silently.

Gone off on that train, no doubt. Well, no matter, he would be picked up. There was one more thing to do.

'Let me have a look at your hands, please.'

Slowly, Alfreda drew off her gloves, then held out her hands.

Coffin looked, then turned away. 'Thank you.'

He was unsurprised by what he had seen, or not seen. No scar. No great surprise. More or less what he had expected. He had never met such a band of liars in his life.

One more layer had peeled off the onion.

He walked down the empty platform and up the tunnel towards the escalator.

As he walked down the dark tunnel, a figure leapt from the bottom of the escalator and fell upon him. They rolled to the ground together. Coffin found himself held in a tight grip. He was a strong man, but his attacker, thin and slender, seemed to have an extra strength.

As he looked in the face which he hardly recognized, teeth drawn back, eyes glittering and the whites flecked with red, he knew why: inside the persona he had known was another one who was now on top.

Hyde had a knife, bright, sharp weapons were his toys. Hyde knew that his function in life was to protect Alfreda, a task which fed him and starved Jekyll. Jekyll was a wimp, Hyde was strong and desperate.

The knife flashed in front of Coffin's eyes. 'Put that knife away, Barney,' he managed to say.

'I'm going to kill you. I am my mother's protector, I am Seth the Protector. I am licensed to kill.'

Is that what he said? Afterwards, Coffin was never quite sure. You can't be sure with a liar and a performer and psychopath.

He tried to push the knife away from his throat, he grasped it, feeling it cut into his fingers.

'She loved me, it was me she attacked her parents for, I saw her bury the bodies. Her and that man she went with.'

Coffin took his fingers from the knife and put his bloody hand over the face because he could not bear to look at it.

'I take it, help arrived,' said Stella, later when they talked at home, cat and dog with them.

'Yes, the uniformed man came with Alfreda and that was

that.' Somehow it had been Alfreda who had controlled her screaming son. 'He was truly terrifying, another person.'

'You are a fool sometimes,' said Stella fondly. 'I could have told you ages ago that he was crooked inside.'

'I wish you had. But how did you know? Don't tell me you guessed.'

'No, of course not, but Alfreda told me when she asked if I would give him a job that he had "troubles". I knew what that meant.' And she nodded her head sagely.

I hope she never does, thought Coffin.

'So what will happen to him?'

Coffin admitted he did not know. 'The courts will decide. Treatment somewhere, I suppose.' But I hope he will not be let loose in the world at large for a long, long time. He added: 'I shall need to talk to him again. On my own if I can do so, he will talk more freely that way. I want to ask him about the use of the card. It couldn't be suicide, those second deaths, so why use that? Just craziness, I suppose.'

'Sometimes people want to shout out,' said Stella. 'And the others? Harry and his brother. Alfreda herself?'

'Harry did not do anything, except arrive here in a strange state of mind . . . I don't know what it will do for his career, not improve it, but that is for the Met to decide. But I know why he seemed so happy: his wife has not left him, the note was to say she was spending a few days with her mother because she was pregnant.'

'Twins?' enquired Stella.

'Too early to say but it's on the cards. It seems to run in families.'

'And what about you? That's a nice clean dressing on your hand.'

'I called on Keith, and his nurse dressed it for me . . . I had to see him, anyway.'

'And?' She raised an eyebrow. 'You've been seeing him a lot lately, haven't you? Come on, you don't think you can hide what was going on from me. The news was good, I take it?'

'Yes, I was worrying over nothing . . . Stress, he tells me, can do all sorts of things to the gut. Today, I feel' – he paused

– 'relieved, hopeful, full of delight . . . Do you think I am suffering from hubris?'

'What's that?'

'Going over the top, I think. Being so triumphant that you incite the gods to strike back.'

Stella held out her arms. 'I won't let it happen.'

'Thank you, darling.' He believed she could do it, too. 'And what about you?'

Stella looked pleased. 'Publicity has been good. Receipts are up. Yes, all is well. We may have to rewire the front of house so that we don't get dim-outs as often as seems to happen.' She looked thoughtful. 'I wonder if that could have been due to Barney?'

'I doubt if he knew much about electric wiring.'

'No.' Stella looked solemn. 'But think of the energy field he must have had in himself.'

'Well, I certainly feel safer with him shut up,' said Coffin.

Incarcerated, Hyde was in excellent spirits. I killed my grand-parents, he thought with gratitude, it was really me that did it. I came back when my mother was not there and saw them all doped up. I saw the suicide note, but I think they were still alive. I pushed a knife up their bums. That'll do you, I thought. They didn't bleed, though. Perhaps you don't from there. Too constipated. Too anally retentive – is that what they say?

I watched Merry and Mum bury the pair, I hid in the bushes. I am good at hiding. Well, it's a necessary skill for me. I disliked Merry, and Harry too when I got to know him. Of course, he didn't attack Stella, I did. It was all pretence me seeing him in the corridor. A lie.

But it wasn't a lie that he looked different that night. I swear his face changed and was more Merry than Harry. God, it chilled me. I thought: that could happen to me.

He withdrew a little from Hyde at that point and became an impersonal observer. There was going to be a third person, or a fourth, depending how you counted.

Hyde, Jekyll, Barney and now Mr Observer.

Let's call him Mr O. This gentleman had considered the

matter of the suicide note on which the fingerprint could be found. He blamed Alfreda in part, because she had kept the note, made her feel better, innocent or more nearly so, and kept it where Hyde knew to find it. No secrets from him.

All the same, Mr O. had to blame Jekyll for its use again, which was stupid. Now Hyde would not have done that, Hyde liked a long life and a rough one. Trust Jekyll, who always wanted to be found out.

That was the worst of being two people, you buggered each other up.

But that was all over for Jekyll, Hyde had triumphed. One extra triumph was demanded, and Mr O. thought of it with relish. Those two could go into retirement, let clever Mr O. take charge. He had plans.

He would get the Chief Commander. He ran his hands over his clothes, a police search had removed a secret knife but there were other weapons.

He held his hands in front of him, how big and strong they were, he would have that man's throat before anyone could stop him. Break his neck.

He looked at the hands. Yes, growing, growing, and the nails too, hooked and powerful, how deep they would tear into the flesh, exposing veins and muscles.

What a pleasure to look forward to.